Rodgers & Hammerstein's
Allegro

Music by
Richard Rodgers

Book & Lyrics by
Oscar Hammerstein II

CONCORD
THEATRICALS

MUSIC AND THIRD-PARTY MATERIALS USE NOTE

IMPORTANT BILLING AND CREDIT REQUIREMENTS

ALLEGRO was first produced at Majestic Theatre in New York, New York on October 10, 1947. The performance was directed and choreographed by Agnes de Mille, with sets and lights by Jo Mielziner, costumes by Lucinda Ballard, music orchestrations by Russell Bennett, music direction by Salvatore Dell'Isola, and dance arragements by Trudi Rittman. The production stage managers were Robert Calley and Herman Kantor. The cast was as follows:

MARJORIE TAYLOR	Annamary Dickey
DR. JOSEPH TAYLOR	William Ching
MAYOR	Edward Platt
GRANDMA TAYLOR	Muriel O'Malley
FRIENDS OF JOEY	Ray Harrison, Frank Westbrook
JENNIE BRINKER	Roberta Jonay
PRINCIPAL	Robert Byrn
MABEL	Evelyn Taylor
BICYCLE BOY	Stanley Simmons
GEORGIE	Harrison Muller
HAZEL	Kathryn Lee
CHARLIE TOWNSEND	John Conte
JOSEPH TAYLOR, JR.	John Battles
MISS LIPSCOMB	Susan Svetlik
CHEER LEADERS	Charles Tate, Sam Steen
COACH	Wilson Smith
NED BRINKER	Paul Parks
ENGLISH PROFESSOR	David Collyer
CHEMISTRY PROFESSOR	William McCully
GREEK PROFESSOR	Raymond Keast
BIOLOGY PROFESSOR	Robert Byrn
PHILOSOPHY PROFESSOR	Blake Ritter
SHAKESPEARE STUDENT	Susan Svetlik
BERTRAM WOOLHAVEN	Ray Harrison
MOLLY	Katrina Van Oss
BEULAH	Gloria Wills
MINISTER	Edward Platt
MILLIE	Julie Humphries
DOT	Sylvia Karlton
ADDIE	Patricia Bybell
DR. BIGBY DENBY	Lawrence Fletcher
MRS. MULHOUSE	Frances Rainer

MRS. LANSDALE . . . . .Lily Paget

JARMAN . . . . Bill Bradley

MAID . . . . Jean Houloose

EMILY . . . . Lisa Kirk

DOORMAN . . . . Tom Perkins

BROOK LANSDALE . . . . Stephen Chase

BUCKLEY . . . . Wilson Smith

SINGERS . . . .
Mary O'Fallon, Charlotte Howard, Lily Paget, Helen Hunter, Sylvia
Karlton, Priscilla Hathaway, Gay Lawrence, Josephine Lambert,
Julie Humphries, Patricia Bybell, Yolanda Renay, Devida Stewart,
Nanette Vezina, Mia Stenn, Lucille Udovick; Glenn Scandur,
Gene Tobin, Walter Kelvin, Bernard Green, David Collyer, Joseph
Caruso, Tommy Barragan, Victor Clarke, Edward Platt, Robert
Reeves, Wilson Smith, Tom Perkins, James Jewell, David Poleri,
Robert Neukum, Raymond Keast, Wesley Swails, Clarence Hali,
Blake Ritter, Ralph Patterson, Robert Byrn, William McCully,
Robert Arnold

DANCERS . . . .
Jean Tachau, Evelyn Taylor, Mariane Oliphant, Patricia Gianinoto,
Andrea Downing, Jean Houloose, Therese Miele, Frances Rainer,
Susan Svetlik, Ruth Ostrander, Patricia Barker; William Bradley,
Daniel Buberniak, Bob Herget, John Laverty, Ralph Linn, Harrison
Muller, Stanley Simmons, Charles Tate, Frank Westbrook, Ralph
Williams, Sam Steen

NOTE: During the Boston try-out the part of MABEL was performed
by Anabelle Lyon and the part of MRS. MULHOUSE by Virginia Poe.

CHARACTERS

(in order of appearance)

MARJORIE TAYLOR
DR. JOSEPH TAYLOR
MAYOR
GRANDMA TAYLOR
FRIENDS OF JOEY
JENNIE BRINKER
PRINCIPAL
GEORGIE
HAZEL SKINNER
CHARLIE TOWNSEND
JOSEPH TAYLOR, JR.
MISS LIPSCOMB
CHEER LEADERS
COACH
NED BRINKER
ENGLISH PROFESSOR
CHEMISTRY PROFESSOR
GREEK PROFESSOR
BIOLOGY PROFESSOR
PHILOSOPHY PROFESSOR
BERTRAM WOOLHAVEN
MOLLY
BEULAH
MINISTER
MILLIE
DOT
ADDIE
DR. BIGBY DENBY
MRS. MULHOUSE
MRS. LANSDALE
JARMAN – a butler
MAID
EMILY WEST
DOORMAN
BROOK LANSDALE
HARRY BUCKLEY

SETTING

The action is set in his home town, his college town, and a large city, all in the same Midwestern state.

There are no stage "sets" in the conventional sense, but backgrounds for action are achieved by small scenic pieces on a moving stage, by light projections, and by drops.

The singing chorus is used frequently to interpret the mental and emotional reactions of the principal characters, after the manner of a Greek chorus. These spoken choral passages may be divided into smaller groups and solos as desired.

TIME

Begins in 1905 on the day Joseph Taylor, Jr. is born, and follows his life to his thirty-fifth year.

AUTHOR'S NOTES

If you are a young physician building up a fashionable practice, is it not important to go to parties given by wealthy patients and to share their social life? When, because of your growing prominence, you are asked to serve on committees for charity drives and to sit on hospital boards, is it not your duty to lend your time and good judgment to these worthy enterprises? Such extra-professional activities establish contacts that help a man's career. They are actually a part of his medical practice. How large a part? An important question.

You will encounter patients who demand production and showmanship from their doctor. They will want unique illnesses and extraordinary remedies – special lamps, freak baths, trips to the South. It's no good sending such people to the drugstore with a prescription for a box of pills. Any two-dollar doctor can prescribe pills. If you want to keep the respect and confidence of this kind of patient you must inject whatever substance the pill would contain into their flanks or rears. This impresses them and feeds their sense of importance. Knowing this, what do you do, doctor? Give the wealthy lady an injection three times a week at twenty dollars a jab? Or tell her the truth and lose her to another doctor down the street? Is there any reason, as long as she is determined to give her money to some doctor, why you shouldn't take it? Whom are you hurting? Her? Her husband? Yourself? Another important question.

Our doctor, Joseph Taylor, Jr., is no Faustian figure beset by the lust for power or pleasure. No transparent Mephistopheles could persuade him to bargain away his soul. Joe would be scared off by the faintest scent of brimstone. But he is given no warning, no time to think or choose. The assault on his integrity is so subtly veiled that a good chunk of it is nibbled away before he knows what is happening to him. It is difficult for a man to recognize the gentle transitions of his own deterioration, the millions of small steps whereby he becomes less and less a doctor, more and more a politician, a promoter, a rhumba dancer, a cocktail-party raconteur, a wet-nurse for spoiled adults – everything but what he started out to be, studied to be, struggled to be.

Mr. Rodgers and I have no wish to imply (as we have been accused of doing) that all city doctors are charlatans and all wealthy people who live in the city are hypochondriacs and greedy neurotics. But there are such people in large cities and they travel in schools, like fish. They use doctors more often than poor people do because they are undeterred by the problem of paying them. They discuss doctors, make them and break them over dinner tables, interchange information and views on one another's symptoms. They like to believe their own cases to be unique and extraordinary, and they gravitate to the physician who will give them the unusual attention such unusual people merit. Thus an anomalous offshoot of medicine grows and thrives in the smart section of a big town. The patients converge into a tribal group, bound together by common interests and presided over by a medicine man who is at once master and servant of them all. This medicine man must supplement his gifts as a doctor by a talent to rationalize the prostitution of those gifts. He must be able to sit up with an insomniac who can't sleep at night because of the self-indulgent life she leads by day, and he must be able to hide from his conscience the knowledge deep in his mind and the feeling deep in his heart that he should be somewhere else, helping sick people who need and deserve him.

Such problems as these are not confined to doctors. An equivalent story could be told about a lawyer, an artist, a businessman, an engineer – anyone who is good at his job. It is a law of our civilization that as soon as a man proves he can contribute to the well-being of the world, there be created an immediate conspiracy to destroy his usefulness, a conspiracy in which he is usually a willing collaborator. Sometimes he awakens to his danger and does something about it. That is the story of *ALLEGRO*. Believing it to be a very typical story, we have told it about a very normal and ordinary boy. There is nothing special or eccentric about him or his family or the town he is born in. He grows up to the accompaniment of the usual joys and sorrows, failures and successes. The girl he marries is a materialist, clever and strong-willed. She is the tragic flaw in Joe's life and the source of his dramatic crisis.

Setting out to tell so simple a tale carries with it an indigenous risk. There is no high drama or broad comedy to lean on. Complete dependence must be placed on one's effort to interest an audience in a group of characters, and interest them to such a degree that they will care about the smallest things that happen to them – everyday things, untheatrical things. In the case of *ALLEGRO*, Mr. Rodgers and I succeeded in this ambition with some critics and failed with others. The majority were on our side. The play has become a solid success, and life would be simple for us if we were content to wallow in the box-office statements, keep rereading the good notices, and dismiss all the bad notices as frivolous and biased droolings of unlearned oafs. It so happens, however, that among the anti-*ALLEGRO* faction are the names of many whose opinions we respect and whose approval we would have cherished. How completely we missed the mark with them while hitting it so squarely with others is a subject worthy of some examination.

It started in Boston. Miss Elinor Hughes of the *Herald* thought our play "a sentimental chronicle, lacking in cohesion and humor, and only intermittently touching." Mr. Elliot Norton of the *Post* found it "romantic, realistic, fantastic, sentimental and gay all at once," and concluded his review by stating, "*ALLEGRO* is the most remarkable musical play I have ever seen."

A few weeks later, the day after the New York opening, Mr. Louis Kronenberger of *PM* rocked us back on our heels with this headline: "Rodgers and Hammerstein Come a Real Cropper." Following this, his two opening sentences were, "*ALLEGRO*, I'm afraid I must say right off, is a very grave disappointment. I'm afraid, in fact, that it can be called an out and out failure." Alongside these lines was a portrait of Mr. Kronenberger, smiling debonairly and looking like a man who isn't afraid to say anything.

Earlier that day, Mr. Howard Barnes in the *Herald Tribune*, had pronounced our play "a consummate theatrical achievement and an electrifying entertainment," and linked it with *SHOW BOAT* and *OKLAHOMA!* Mr. William Hawkins, of the evening *World-Telegram*, described the play as "lacking in visual excitement and theatrical stimulation." Mr. Morehouse, of the evening *Sun*, referring to the same performance of the same play, called it "distinguished and tumultuous," "excitingly unconventional," "a play of beauty and dignity, produced with perception and imagination." Mr. John Chapman in the *News* found us too serious-minded, but Mr. Brooks Atkinson of the *Times*, speaking of the first act (which he liked better than the second), said that it was "full of a kind of unexploited glory" and felt that we had "just missed the final splendor of a perfect work of art."

So went the series of bewildering conflicting thoughts and feelings. Mr. Robert Coleman, in the *Mirror*, gave us his blessing with a gorgeous headline: "*ALLEGRO* Is Perfect and Great." Mr. Richard Watts, Jr., of the *Post*, was on our side, too. Mr. Robert Garland, of the evening *Journal-American* said that the play belied its title because it was not played at an allegro pace. Bob seemed to feel somewhat like the farmer in the old Chic Sale story who, after attending a play entitled *THE LION AND THE MOUSE* wanted his money back "because there wasn't an animal in the troupe."

For a playwright to debate the virtues of his work with a critic is an undignified and fruitless proceeding. A critic goes to a play and likes it or doesn't. His reasons may be many and deep. His expression of them may be accurate or not. But the relation of the play to him or to anyone is the audience is an essentially emotional one. The intellectual justification for an emotional reaction may be interesting, but it is far less important than the reaction itself.

One line of comment that bobbed up in several criticisms surprised us very much. We were chided for ascribing only virtues to small town folk and only wickedness and vice to the people of the great cities. We, of course, intended no such conclusion to be drawn from our play. In the chapter-and-verse department we can quote this dialogue from Act II:

EMILY. *(The nurse, speaking to* **JOE**, *the doctor.)* Getting sour on rich city people?

JOE. No, I'm not, Emily. There's nothing wrong with people just because they have money or live in the city – nothing wrong with being a city doctor – but this crowd that we get!

As far as small-town virtue is concerned, the girl Joe marries, born and brought up in the same small town, is a crass and vicious little baggage. Her father, another rural figure, is a smug Babbit, and the wedding guests in the country church are as catty a crowd of gossips as can be found.

Our best defense is the answer made for us by Mr. Arthur Pollock of the *Brooklyn Eagle*. After a brief synopsis of the plot he said, "The most frequent criticism of this is that Mr. Hammerstein is saying that the only real way to live is in a little place and that the big cities are wicked. I don't believe that is what he is saying at all, though he might have said with more point what I suppose him to mean. And that is that our values are too often false, that we are too eager to worship large scale success, that we run away from ourselves in search of bright excitements, that we think we are happy when we are only making a noise and pretending to be gay, that we believe all is gold that glitters and worship the phoney, that we care less about being useful citizens than about being big shots.

"If that is not what he means he would not have called this big, plain and beautiful musical play *ALLEGRO*. For the satirical song 'Allegro' in the last act, states his theme, that when we think we are dancing to the tune with an allegro beat, 'brisk, lively, merry and bright,' we are simply living in a kind of Benzedrine dream that has no relation to reality. We're kidding ourselves. And this is true whether we live in a big city or a small town. It just happens that in a big city we make a greater fuss about it because there are more of us.

"At any rate, there is in *ALLEGRO* more simple loveliness and true feeling than it has ever before been possible to experience in the presence of an American musical play. The theater will never be the same again because of it."

There is one other general line of criticism upon which I should like to comment. It has been said that I wrote a "radio script," a kind of soap opera, filled with trite characters and situations. This is entirely true. A story like this must, of its very nature, be built of familiar material. There is no novelty in *ALLEGRO* except its style of presentation.

When an old problem is discussed, it is an easy thing to say, "We've heard all that before." But hearing it all before has done no good if one hasn't learned anything from what he has heard. If men are continuing to squander their time and usefulness for the wrong things, it would seem important to point this out to them. That is the simple reason why *ALLEGRO* was written. If you don't like that reason, you won't like *ALLEGRO*.

Oscar Hammerstein II
Doylestown, PA
January 12, 1948

MUSICAL NUMBERS

ACT I

"Overture" . . . . Orchestra

"Joseph Taylor, Jr." . . . . Ensemble

"I Know It Can Happen Again" . . . . Grandma

"One Foot, Other Foot" . . . . Ensemble

"Winters Go By" . . . . Grandma Taylor & Ensemble

"Poor Joe" . . . . Ensemble

"A Fellow Needs a Girl" . . . . Dr. Taylor & Marjorie

"Freshman Dance" . . . . Ensemble

"A Darn Nice Campus" . . . . Joe

"Wildcats" . . . . Joe & Ensemble

"Jenny Reads Letter" . . . . Jennie

"So Far" . . . . Beulah

"You Are Never Away" . . . . Joe & Ensemble

"Poor Joe – Reprise" . . . . Ensemble

"What a Lovely Day For a Wedding" . . . . Ned & Ensemble

"It May Be a Good Idea for Joe" . . . . Charlie

"Finale Act I" . . . . Orchestra

"Winters Go By – Reprise" . . . . Grandma Taylor

"To Have and to Hold" . . . . Marjorie & Ensemble

"Wish Them Well" . . . . Company

ACT II

"Entr'acte" . . . . Orchestra

"Money Isn't Everything" . . . . Millie, Dot, Addie, Hazel & Jennie

"Poor Joe – Reprise" . . . . Ensemble

"Change of Scene (You Are Never Away – Reprise)" . . . . Joe

"Incidental (A Fellow Needs a Girl – Reprise)" . . . . Marjorie

"Yatata, Yatata, Yatata" . . . . Charlie & Company

"The Gentleman is a Dope" . . . . Emily

"Allegro" . . . . Charlie, Emily, Joe & Ensemble

"Come Home" . . . . Marjorie & Ensemble

"Finale Ultimo" . . . . Company

It is a law of our civilization that as soon as a man proves he can contribute to the well-being of the world, there be created an immediate conspiracy to destroy his usefulness, a conspiracy in which he is usually a willing collaborator. Sometimes he awakens to his danger and does something about it. That is the story of ALLEGRO.

Oscar Hammerstein II

ACT I

[MUSIC NO. 00 "OVERTURE"]

Scene One:
Marjorie's Bedroom

(As in all the succeeding scenes, there is no detailed stage set – no walls, no windows, no other furniture except the bed itself.)

[MUSIC NO. 01 "OPENING (JOSEPH TAYLOR, JR.)"]

*(The lights come up slowly and are concentrated only on the bed where **MARJORIE** lies, looking dreamily contented. Soon another light comes up on the opposite side of the stage, revealing an **ENSEMBLE GROUP**.)*

ENSEMBLE.
THE LADY IN BED IS MARJORIE TAYLOR,
DOCTOR JOSEPH TAYLOR'S WIFE.

SOLO SOPRANO.
EXCEPT FOR THE DAY WHEN SHE MARRIED JOE,
THIS IS THE HAPPIEST DAY OF HER LIFE!

ENSEMBLE.
EXCEPT FOR THE DAY WHEN SHE MARRIED JOE,
THIS IS THE HAPPIEST DAY OF HER LIFE!

TAYLOR. *(Entering.)* You awake, dear?

1

MARJORIE. Where've you been, Joe?

TAYLOR. *(Putting down his doctor's bag.)* Making rounds.
You were asleep when I left. How do you feel?

MARJORIE. Feel like jumping out of bed and dancing.

TAYLOR. Well, don't.

> *(He kisses her.)*

How's old Skeezicks?

> *(Gently he lifts the bedcover beside* **MARJORIE.***)*

MARJORIE. Old Skeezicks is asleep.

> *(**MARJORIE** and **TAYLOR** gaze down fondly at their first born.)*

MEN. *(Soft and staccato.)*
HIS HAIR IS FUZZY, HIS EYES ARE BLUE.
HIS EYES MAY CHANGE – THEY OFTEN DO.
HE WEIGHS EIGHT POUNDS AND AN OUNCE OR TWO –
JOSEPH TAYLOR, JUNIOR!

WOMEN.
WHEN HE WAKES UP HE WANTS TO EAT,
AND WHEN HE SLEEPS HE WETS HIS SEAT,
BUT YOU'D FORGIVE ANYONE AS SWEET
AS JOSEPH TAYLOR, JUNIOR!

> *(**TAYLOR** takes a thermometer out of his pocket.)*

MARJORIE. Do many people know yet?

TAYLOR. About him?

> *(He shakes the thermometer as doctors do.)*

Do they know! Why the whole town's in an uproar!

(He puts the thermometer in her mouth and sits on the bed, speaking with extravagant gestures.)

Women are rushing to church! Men are pouring into the saloons! Early this morning the townspeople gathered in front of Elks Hall! His Honor the Mayor addressed them!

(The **ENSEMBLE GROUP** *scatters and runs out to join others who now come out from all sides, shouting and chattering excitedly.)*

GIRL. Have you heard the news?

(Streamers of confetti are projected on the backdrop.)

ANOTHER GIRL. It's a boy!

ALDERMAN. *(Quieting the* **CROWD.***)* Hear ye! Hear ye!

(The façade of Elks Hall is projected on the backdrop.)

MAYOR. The birthday of Joseph Taylor, Jr. is bound to be a legal holiday someday, so we might as well start on his first birthday. Close the bank!

(Cheers.)

And tell the kids no school today!

(Cheers from the **KIDS.***)*

MOXIE MAN. *(Entering with Moxie wagon.)* Moxie – Free Moxie – Free Moxie –

(A group of **DRUNKS** *reel on, singing.)*

DRUNKS.
HIS HAIR IS FUZZY, HIS EYES ARE BLUE.
HIS EYES MAY CHANGE – THEY OFTEN DO.

HE WEIGHS EIGHT POUNDS AND AN OUNCE OR TWO –
JOSEPH TAYLOR – (HIC) – JUNIOR!

> *(The **DRUNKS** stop and take off their hats reverently as a church **CHOIR** walks on slowly.)*

CHOIR.
RING OUT, RING OUT, OH BELLS OF JOY,
AND ALL THE SHIPS AT SEA, AHOY!
THE DOCTOR'S WIFE HAS A BOUNCING BOY,
JOSEPH TAYLOR, JUNIOR!

CHILDREN. *(Lifting high their exalted and very squeaky voices.)*
SEE WHAT MRS. TAYLOR'S DONE!
HAD HERSELF AN EIGHT POUND SON!
HAIL HIM, HAIL HIM EV'RYONE!
JOSEPH TAYLOR, JUNIOR!

ENSEMBLE.
JOSEPH TAYLOR, JUNIOR!
RING, OH BELLS OF JOY
FOR JOSEPH TAYLOR, JUNIOR,
MARJORIE'S EIGHT-POUND BOY!

> *(Their impressive vocal climax attained, a curtain is drawn in front of them, leaving only **MARJORIE** in her bed, with **TAYLOR** beside her.)*

TAYLOR.
JOSEPH TAYLOR, JUNIOR,
MARJORIE'S EIGHT POUND BOY!

> *(With a flourish, he takes the thermometer out of her mouth.)*

MARJORIE. *(Laughing.)* You fool!

GRANDMA. *(Offstage.)* Joe! *(Nearer.)* Joe!

TAYLOR. Here I am, Mother.

GRANDMA. *(Entering.)* Ned Brinker just drove up in his buckboard. He says Jennie has started and you better go right over there with him. Don't forget you got to stop in to see Old Man McCoy too. That's on your way back.

TAYLOR. Gosh! Is everybody going to have their babies today? *(Testify.)* This town needs about ten more doctors.

> *(Picking up his satchel.)*

I wish old Skeezicks would hurry and grow up so's he could help me.

> *(He takes another peek at the baby.)*

MARJORIE. What makes you think he's going to be a doctor?

TAYLOR. I dunno. He...he looks like a doctor.

> *(He kisses her and starts out, calling back over his shoulder.)*

See that the old lady gets a rest, Mother.

> *(He exits.)*

GRANDMA. I'll take the young man into his crib.

> *(She picks tip the baby, holding him up high on her shoulder.)*

Oops! Did you hear that?

MARJORIE. What?

GRANDMA. He brought up a bubble.

MARJORIE. Isn't he clever!

GRANDMA. That's Grandma's good boy!

MARJORIE. Mother Taylor –

GRANDMA. What?

MARJORIE. Do you think he'll ever get to look any better?

GRANDMA. Sure he will. He'll look younger when he's older.

> *(**MARJOIE**'s bed goes off and **GRANDMA** carries the baby to a bassinet, placing him in it tenderly.)*

You don't look any worse than your father did when he was a baby. Maybe you will grow up to be a doctor like him. But looking at you now, it doesn't seem possible.

[MUSIC NO. 02 "I KNOW IT CAN HAPPEN AGAIN"]

STARTING OUT, SO FOOLISHLY SMALL,
IT'S HARD TO BELIEVE YOU WILL GROW AT ALL.
IT'S HARD TO BELIEVE THAT THINGS LIKE YOU
CAN EVER TURN OUT TO BE MEN,
BUT I'VE SEEN IT HAPPEN BEFORE,
SO I KNOW IT CAN HAPPEN AGAIN.
FOOD AND SLEEP, AND PLENTY OF SOAP,
MOLASSES AND SULFUR, AND LOVE, AND HOPE –
THE WINTERS GO BY, THE SUMMERS FLY,
AND ALL OF A SUDDEN YOU'RE MEN!
I HAVE SEEN IT HAPPEN BEFORE
AND I KNOW IT CAN HAPPEN AGAIN.
AND I KNOW IT CAN HAPPEN AGAIN.
(Optional cut.) AND I KNOW IT CAN HAPPEN AGAIN.

> *(The lights dim on her. Loud voices are heard.)*

MAN'S VOICE. Pretty baby! Close your eyes and go to sleep.

WOMAN'S VOICE. Open your eyes. Say goo goo!

(An **ENSEMBLE GROUP** *has entered.)*

ENSEMBLE. *(Speaking in unison.)* A funny plane to be coming to in life.

> *(They speak straight out at the audience and in the ensuing sequences the audience is made to feel that it is* **JOSEPH TAYLOR, JR.,** *experiencing the first stages of consciousness and then being whirled through the swift adventures of his infancy and childhood.)*

MAN'S VOICE. Papa's boy!

WOMAN'S VOICE. Mama's precious! Grandma's good boy! Say goo goo! Coochie, coochie, coochie.

MAN'S VOICE. Wanna play with the rattle?

> *(The sound of a rattle is heard, very loud, followed by the sharp, protesting wail of a baby.)*

WOMAN'S VOICE. Coochie, coochie, coochie.

> *(A large head is projected on the backdrop.)*

ENSEMBLE. It's a funny place.
And those things with the big heads
Don't help to clear things up.
Nobody helps you.
You have to puzzle it out for yourself.

GRANDMA'S VOICE. Ipecac...ipecac.

ENSEMBLE. Now there's a sound you've begun to know.
It means they try to put something into your mouth.

> *(A large spoon is seen on the backdrop.)*

Sometimes you give them a fight.

> *(Sound of a baby's wail.)*

You spit it out.

But they keep giving you more.

MARJORIE. *(Entering.)* Open your mouth for Mother. That's a good boy.

ENSEMBLE. Another sound you're getting to know.

A face goes with it.

MARJORIE. *(Looking out at audience.)* Please, Joey. Like a good boy.

ENSEMBLE. All right.

Might as well take, the darn stuff –

If *she* wants you to.

MARJORIE. That's Mother's beautiful, big, brave man!

ENSEMBLE. Knows how to make you feel good, that one.

TAYLOR. *(Entering, putting his arm around* **MARJORIE** *and talking straight out at the audience.)* That's how they get you, Skeezicks! Call you their big, brave, beautiful man. That's how they make you do all the things you don't want to do – take your ipecac, comb your hair, buy them wedding rings...

ENSEMBLE. You're getting to know that one, too –

The one with the loud, rough voice.

When he holds you against him

He doesn't feel soft like the other one.

He doesn't smell as sweet, either.

TAYLOR. Well, so long, you two. Got to go out and kill a few patients.

(He picks up his bag.)

ENSEMBLE. He's leaving.

When he picks up that black thing

He always goes.

*(**TAYLOR** takes **MARJORIE** in his arms and kisses her.)*

Look! He's hurting the little one!

Don't let him do that!

Stop him!

> *(The sound of a baby's wail;* **TAYLOR** *releases* **MARJORIE** *quickly.)*

MARJORIE. *(Laughing, talking to audience.)* What's the matter, Joey? Are you crying because your daddy is going?

TAYLOR. Take it easy, Skeezicks. I'll be back soon.

> *(He exits.)*

ENSEMBLE. There he goes… Good!

> *(***MARJORIE*** *waves upstage through imaginary window.)*

Look!

She's waving at the big one!

Why does she do that?

Why isn't she looking at *you* instead of him?

Make her look at you!

> *(A loud wail;* **MARJORIE** *turns.)*

That's getting her!

> *(A louder wail;* **MARJORIE** *comes forward anxiously.)*

You've got her!

> *(The lights go out on* **MARJORIE**.*)*

[MUSIC NO. 03 "PUDGY LEGS"]

ENSEMBLE.

PUDGY LEGS BEGIN TO GROW LONG

AND ONE SUNNY DAY, WHEN YOU'RE FEELING STRONG,

YOU STRAIGHTEN A KNEE AND SUDDENLY
YOU'RE STRUCK WITH A DARING IDEA!

>   (**GRANDMA** *enters and stands transfixed,*
>   *fascinated by something she sees as she looks*
>   *straight out at the audience. She calls off in a*
>   *hoarse whisper.*)

GRANDMA. Marjorie!

>   (**MARJORIE** *runs on, looks out, and stops,*
>   *astounded. She whispers to* **GRANDMA.**)

MARJORIE. He's standing up!

>   (*A sudden look of worry on her face and pity*
>   *in her voice.*)

Ah! He fell down!

>   (*She starts forward but* **GRANDMA** *stops her.*)

GRANDMA. Let him try to get up by himself.

MARJORIE. Come on, Joey. Try again.

ENSEMBLE. Wonder if she knows how dangerous it is!
You're sorry you started now.
What got into you today, anyway?
All of a sudden crawling wasn't good enough!
Well, there they are watching you.
Go to it!

GRANDMA. That's Grandma's good boy!

ENSEMBLE. Grandma's good boy!
But what do you do now that you're up?
As usual, nobody helps.
You've got to puzzle everything out for yourself...
Whoops!
Almost fell again.

Hey! Wait!

Do you realize what happened just then?

> *(The voices of the **ENSEMBLE** are charged with the excitement of discovery.)*

You felt yourself falling

And you put one foot out to save yourself,

And you didn't fall!

Say! Maybe if you keep taking steps,

One after the other,

One after the other –

Maybe going forward is easier than standing still!

(Slowly and significantly.) Maybe going forward is easier than standing still!

Come on!

Step out!

> *(**MARJORIE** and **GRANDMA** in unison with the **ENSEMBLE** plead and exhort while projections on the drop convey the thrills of **JOEY**'s hazardous trip.)*

One foot, other foot,

One foot, other foot,

One foot, other foot...

Faster

Faster

Faster

Faster

Ah-h-h-h-h-h-h-h!

> *(The lights go out on **MARJORIE** and **GRANDMA** as they open their arms to catch **JOEY**. The **ENSEMBLE** spreads out across the stage and sings, to express **JOEY**'s first big conquest.)*

[MUSIC NO. 04 "ONE FOOT, OTHER FOOT"]

ONE FOOT, OTHER FOOT,
ONE FOOT, OTHER FOOT...

NOW YOU CAN GO WHEREVER YOU WANT,
WHEREVER YOU WANT TO GO.
ONE FOOT OUT AND THE OTHER FOOT OUT –
THAT'S ALL YOU NEED TO KNOW!

NOW YOU CAN DO WHATEVER YOU WANT,
WHATEVER YOU WANT TO DO.
HERE YOU ARE IN A WONDERFUL WORLD
ESPECIALLY MADE FOR YOU,
ESPECIALLY MADE FOR YOU!

NOW YOU CAN MARCH AROUND THE YARD,
SHOUT TO ALL THE NEIGHBORHOOD,
TELL THE FOLKS YOU'RE FEELING GOOD –
FOLKS OUGHT TO KNOW WHEN BOYS FEEL GOOD!

NOW YOU CAN IMITATE A DOG.
CHASE A BIRD AROUND A TREE.
YOU CAN CHASE A BUMBLE BEE.
ONCE IS ENOUGH TO CHASE A BEE!

NOW YOU CAN PLAY AMONG THE FLOW'RS.
GRAB YOURSELF A HUNK O' DIRT.
SMUDGE IT ON YOUR MOTHER'S SKIRT.
THAT LITTLE DIRT WON'T HURT A SKIRT!

ONE FOOT, OTHER FOOT,
ONE FOOT, OTHER FOOT...

(Singing with mounting triumph.)

NOW YOU CAN DO WHATEVER YOU WANT,
WHATEVER YOU WANT TO DO.
HERE YOU ARE IN A WONDERFUL WORLD
ESPECIALLY MADE FOR YOU.
ESPECIALLY MADE FOR YOU!

WOMEN.
ESPECIALLY MADE FOR YOU
TO WALK IN, TO RUN IN,
TO PLAY IN THE SUN IN.

MEN.
ESPECIALLY MADE FOR YOU.
FOR NOW YOU CAN WALK,
YOU TAUGHT YOURSELF TO WALK!
YOU PUZZLED IT OUT YOURSELF
AND NOW YOU CAN WALK!

ALL. One foot, other foot,
One foot, other foot,
One foot, other foot,
One foot, other foot...

NOW YOU CAN GO WHEREVER YOU WANT,
WHEREVER YOU WANT TO GO!
ONE FOOT OUT AND THE OTHER FOOT OUT,
ONE FOOT OUT AND THE OTHER FOOT OUT,
ONE FOOT OUT AND THE OTHER FOOT OUT
AND THE WORLD BELONGS TO JOE!
AND THE WORLD BELONGS TO JOE!

(After the applause, the **ENSEMBLE** *begins to exit.)*

ENSEMBLE.
NOW YOU CAN IMITATE A DOG.
CHASE A BIRD AROUND A TREE.
YOU CAN CHASE A BUMBLE BEE.
ONCE IS ENOUGH TO CHASE A BEE!

(Direct segue into:)

[MUSIC NO. 05 "CHILDREN'S DANCE"]

(Now the **DANCING ENSEMBLE**, *representing* **JOEY***'s playmates, scamper on, shouting,*

romping, playing children's games, "growing up" exuberantly. In the course of this ballet a new principal character is introduced – "Joey Taylor's girl," **JENNIE BRINKER.** *She tries to emulate the feats of the tomboy girls, but she loses her nerve. She then resorts to dancing for the* **BOYS,** *striking pretty poses and flattering them. She is that kind of "girly" girl and always will be. At the end of the ballet the light dims, the* **CHILDREN** *bid one another good night and drift away.* **GRANDMA** *enters, troubled, trying to smile in spite of her worry.)*

GIRLS.

TRALLALALA, LA, LA, LA, LA, LA.

TRALLALALA, LA, LA, LA, LA, LA.

GRANDMA.

FOOD AND SLEEP, AND PLENTY OF SOAP,

MOLASSES AND SULFUR, AND LOVE, AND HOPE –

THE WINTERS GO BY, THE SUMMERS FLY...

...AND ALL OF A SUDDEN...

(A cloud crosses her face.)

...ALL OF A SUDDEN...

(She exits. The lights change, becoming bright again. **TWO BOYS** *run on and shout out to the audience.)*

FIRST BOY. C'mon out, Joey. Race you down to the picture house.

SECOND BOY. Jo-ey! It's a Bronco Billy!

ENSEMBLE. But you can't go today.

FIRST BOY. Gee! That's right. I forgot – *(Whispering to* **SECOND BOY.***)* his grandma!

SECOND BOY. Oh, yeah. Gee!

> *(They wave timidly and walk away.)*

[MUSIC NO. 05A "GRANDMOTHER'S DEATH"]

> *(**TAYLOR** enters, putting on his Mack gloves.)*

TAYLOR. Ready, Marge?

MARJORIE. *(Entering.)* Yes, darling. *(Speaking to audience.)* Joey, stay in the house till we get back, like a good boy. *(To **TAYLOR**.)* Ned Brinker's bringing little Jennie over to keep him company.

TAYLOR. That's good. These things are nothing for kids. Nothing for anybody. *(His voice breaks huskily.)* She was a good old lady, wasn't she?

> *(**MARJORIE** takes his arm and they go off. An **ENSEMBLE GROUP** enters on the right; **GRANDMA** is among them.)*

ENSEMBLE. "These things are nothing for kids..."
But it *did* happen to you.
You're a kid,
And yet here you are,
And suddenly you have no Grandma.

GRANDMA. It'll be funny without me. Hard to imagine the house without me.

JENNIE. *(Entering, carrying a rag doll and candy apples in a paper bag.)* G'morning, Joseph. I'm sorry about your grandma.

> *(She sits down, takes two candy apples from the paper bag, compares them, then offers the smaller to **JOE**. He is apparently not interested. She withdraws it and starts licking the other one.)*

GRANDMA. Death is a sad thing. People cry and sob, grown people. You haven't seen your father cry. He just looks kind of angry.

ENSEMBLE. Grandma was his mother – gosh! Suppose your mother ever... Oh, well *that* isn't going to happen. Just stop thinking like that! Get back to Grandma, quick!

[MUSIC NO. 06 "WINTERS GO BY"]

GRANDMA. Look out, Joey. Your eyes are watery. Blow your nose.

> (**JENNIE** *holds out her handkerchief.*)

If Jennie sees you crying, she'll cry too. Try to smile. Ah – that's Grandma's good boy.

> (**JENNIE** *smiles and puts her handkerchief away. Then she gets up and goes off as the* **ENSEMBLE** *starts to sing.* **GRANDMA** *retires soon after.*)

ENSEMBLE.
THE WINTERS GO BY, THE SUMMERS FLY
AND SOON YOU'RE A STUDENT IN "HIGH"!
AND NOW YOUR CLOTHES ARE SPOTLESSLY CLEAN,
YOUR HEAD IS ANOINTED WITH BRILLIANTINE!
YOU'RE BRIMMING WITH HOPE,
BUT CAN'T QUITE COPE
WITH PROBLEMS THAT VEX AND PERPLEX,
FOR YOU DON'T QUITE KNOW HOW TO TREAT
THE BEWILDERING OPPOSITE SEX!

> (**JENNIE** *enters. She is sixteen now and wears a party dress. She faces the audience.*)

JENNIE. G'night, Joseph. I had a lovely time...er...g'night.

(She looks up with an expression that would make it obvious to a more sophisticated escort that she expected to be kissed.)

ENSEMBLE. *(Whispering.)* What do you suppose Jennie would do if you kissed her?

JENNIE. *(Putting all the sex she can into her voice.)* G'night.

[MUSIC NO. 07 "POOR JOE"]

ENSEMBLE.

POOR JOE,
THE OLDER YOU GROW
THE HARDER IT IS TO KNOW
WHAT TO THINK,
WHAT TO DO,
WHERE TO GO!

JENNIE. Well...g'night, Joseph.

ENSEMBLE. Jennie is so innocent, so frail! You could crush her in your strong, manly arms...but that wouldn't be right. Besides, she might get sore – might yell, and wake up her old man!

JENNIE. *(In a flat, discouraged voice.)* Yeah. See you in school tomorrow.

(The light fades on a girl with a frustrated heart and a disgusted face.)

ENSEMBLE. Heigh-ho! It would have been nice... Think about it as you walk home. Make believe you did it, and make out she wasn't mad when you kissed her. Gee, wouldn't it be wonderful if girls liked it too!

[MUSIC NO. 08 "DIPLOMA"]

YOUR LOVE FOR JENNIE BECOMES MORE KEEN,
YOUR ARMS GET LONG, YOUR LEGS GET LEAN,
AND ALL AT ONCE YOU ARE SEVENTEEN!

SCHOOL PRINCIPAL. *(Stepping out from* ENSEMBLE, *a sealed and ribboned diploma in his hand.)*
JOSEPH TAYLOR, JUNIOR!

> *(He hands the diploma out toward the audience; lights fade.)*

Scene Two:
The Taylors' Porch

(TAYLOR and MARJORIE sit side by side in the moonlight. She is darning socks.)

TAYLOR. *(Looking out and up.)* Do you suppose he's asleep?

MARJORIE. *(Pointing up toward height of theater's balcony as if at another wing or ell of their house.)* Must be. His light's out.

JOE'S VOICE. I'm too excited to be asleep, leaving for college in the morning. Leaving home –

TAYLOR. *(To MARJORIE.)* Don't look so mopey. The boy isn't going away forever.

MARJORIE. You're not his mother.

TAYLOR. That's the most unnecessary statement you've made this year.

MARJORIE. You know very well what I mean, Joseph Taylor. I'm losing him. When he comes back from college he'll be a different boy. I won't know him.

TAYLOR. I'll point him out to you.

MARJORIE. *(Ignoring this as husband humor.)* I've had this feeling – all the time I was getting his things ready, sewing his name on his shirts, helping him pack. "This is the end of me," I thought. Mother's job is over.

JOE'S VOICE. If I closed my window they'd know I heard all that! Anyway, I'm too interested to stop listening. They're talking about me. Gee, I'm pretty important to them!

MARJORIE. *(Who has been studying TAYLOR.)* You look kind of mopey yourself.

TAYLOR. I had another tough day.

MARJORIE. How's Mrs. Mason doing?

TAYLOR. Worse since yesterday.

MARJORIE. *(Fully understanding what this means to him.)* Ah, Joe! And last night you came home and said you thought you had the case licked.

TAYLOR. *(Sighing.)* That's what I thought.

MARJORIE. You'll pull her through. I have a feeling.

TAYLOR. Well, Marge – I'll tell this to *you* – at this moment I haven't the faintest idea what to do for the old lady. Every diagnosis I've made so far I've had to throw out. I tell you I'm stumped.

MARJORIE. *(Putting her hand on his.)* You'll beat it. I have a feeling about it.

JOE. I've been hearing this kind of talk ever since I can remember. Dad always has one case that stumps him, and Mother always has a "feeling" he'll beat it.

MARJORIE. Do you think Joe takes to medicine?

TAYLOR. He's a born doctor! Could tell when he made rounds with me this summer. Could tell by the questions he asked, by the way he looked when he asked them.

MARJORIE. He was telling me how he helped you with the Jacobs boy.

TAYLOR. Yep. That was a quick one.

JOE'S VOICE. Dad had to use the kitchen table to operate on the kid. Boy, was I scared! Nothing in the world mattered except saving a ten-year-old boy I'd never seen before. Gosh! Who would want to be anything else but a doctor!

MARJORIE. How you coming along with the hospital fund?

TAYLOR. I don't know, Marge. It's hard raising money when people can give you only five and ten dollar gifts – some of 'em give fifty cents.

MARJORIE. You'll have your hospital some day, Joe. I just know it.

TAYLOR. *(Smiling at her.)* Got a feeling about it?

MARJORIE. Yes. I have a feeling.

TAYLOR. I hope Joe marries a girl who gets "feelings" about things.

MARJORIE. I hope he gets a girl with good sense.

TAYLOR. Y-y-yes. Good sense is all right too, if she doesn't overdo it... D'you suppose he'll marry Jennie Brinker?

MARJORIE. Oh, it's hard to say. He'll be meeting a lot of new girls at college.

JOE'S VOICE. But not like Jennie! No other girl could ever be like her. She's so...unusual!

TAYLOR. I hope he doesn't pick a lemon. It's only dumb luck when a boy picks the right girl – the way I did.

MARJORIE. You say that to make me feel good.

TAYLOR. Well, doesn't it?

[MUSIC NO. 09 "A FELLOW NEEDS A GIRL"]

MARJORIE. *(Laughing.)* Fool!

TAYLOR.

A FELLOW NEEDS A GIRL
TO SIT BY HIS SIDE
AT THE END OF A WEARY DAY,
TO SIT BY HIS SIDE
AND LISTEN TO HIM TALK
AND AGREE WITH THE THINGS HE'LL SAY.

A FELLOW NEEDS A GIRL
TO HOLD IN HIS ARMS
WHEN THE REST OF THE WORLD GOES WRONG,
TO HOLD IN HIS ARMS
AND KNOW THAT SHE BELIEVES

THAT HER FELLOW IS WISE AND STRONG.

WHEN THINGS GO RIGHT
AND HIS JOB'S WELL DONE,
HE WANTS TO SHARE
THE PRIZE HE'S WON.
IF NO ONE SHARES,
AND NO ONE CARES,
WHERE'S THE FUN
OF A JOB WELL DONE
OR A PRIZE YOU'VE WON?

A FELLOW NEEDS A HOME,
HIS OWN KIND OF HOME,
BUT TO MAKE THIS DREAM COME TRUE
A FELLOW NEEDS A GIRL,
HIS OWN KIND OF GIRL –
MY KIND OF GIRL IS YOU.

> *(The music continues. The light remains on* **MARJORIE** *and* **TAYLOR** *as they sit contentedly together.)*

JOE'S VOICE. They're funny when they're by themselves – not like a mother and father. A fellow and a girl – like Jennie and me – almost.

MARJORIE.

MY FELLOW NEEDS A GIRL
TO SIT BY HIS SIDE
AT THE END OF A WEARY DAY,
SO I SIT BY HIS SIDE
AND LISTEN TO HIM TALK
AND AGREE WITH THE THINGS HE'LL SAY.

MY FELLOW NEEDS A GIRL
TO HOLD IN HIS ARMS
WHEN THE REST OF THE WORLD GOES WRONG,
TO HOLD IN HIS ARMS
AND KNOW THAT SHE BELIEVES

THAT HER FELLOW IS WISE AND STRONG.

WHEN THINGS GO RIGHT
AND HIS JOB'S WELL DONE,
HE WANTS TO SHARE
THE PRIZE HE'S WON.
IF NO ONE SHARES,
AND NO ONE CARES,
WHERE'S THE FUN
OF A JOB WELL DONE?

TAYLOR.
OR A PRIZE YOU'VE WON?

MARJORIE.
MY FELLOW NEEDS A HOME,
HIS OWN KIND OF HOME,
BUT TO MAKE HIS DREAMS COME TRUE,

TAYLOR.
A FELLOW NEEDS TO LOVE,

MARJORIE.
HIS ONE ONLY LOVE –

TAYLOR & MARJORIE.
MY ONLY LOVE IS YOU.

(The lights fade.)

[MUSIC NO. 10 "FRESHMEN GET TOGETHER"]

*(Drums begin and underscore **JOE**'s line.)*

JOE'S VOICE. *(In the darkness.)* Dear Mother and Dad: Tonight I am going to the Freshman Get Together Dance in the college gym.

(Strains of a jazz band steal in.)

Scene Three:
The College Gym

(Japanese lanterns are projected on the backdrop. A tacky crowd of **BOYS** *and* **GIRLS***, gauche but gay, give some painful illustrations of what were considered snappy dance steps in 1921. Presently they come to a sudden stop and stand still in a frozen picture.)*

ENSEMBLE. *(Addressing the audience.)* This is how we look when we are dancing –

But we feel much better than we look.

We feel that we are floating and flying.

Look at our dreamy faces!

Here is how we think we are dancing.

(Direct segue into:)

[MUSIC NO. 11 "DREAM SEQUENCE"]

(They move again, but now the **DANCERS** *float and fly as they imagine they were doing. The gymnasium lanterns become silver stars and planets in a dazzling firmament. The clothes of the* **DANCERS** *are filmy and graceful, the Dixieland Jazz Band now sounds like a symphony orchestra. Direct segue into:)*

[MUSIC NO. 12 "ANNABELLE SOLO"]

(Direct segue into:)

[MUSIC NO. 13 "END OF COLLEGE DANCE"]

(After several minutes of this fulfilled illusion the picture dissolves back to the way it was – accomplished by substitution

of **DANCERS** – *the gymnasium lanterns are back, the Dixieland jazz blares out again.)*

VOICE. You are about to get your first look at yourself. Joseph Taylor, Jr. is one of these boys. Shall we try to pick him out?

(A spotlight is turned on a likely looking **COUPLE.***)*

GIRL. What're you going to be when you get out of college?

CHARLIE TOWNSEND. I don't know. A doctor, I guess. What're you going to be when you get out of college?

GIRL. I don't go to college. I just came up for the dance.

CHARLIE. Well, what're you going to be anyway?

GIRL. I don't know. Somebody's wife, I guess.

CHARLIE. How'd you like to be a doctor's wife?

GIRL. You've got some line, Charlie.

(They dance off.)

VOICE. Charlie? Well, let's try another.

(The spotlight is turned to a fancy **DANCING COUPLE.** *The* **BOY** *is too fancy for his partner's taste.)*

GIRL. *(Struggling to yank herself free.)* You're the limit! Stop it! You're pulling me to pieces! Georgie! Stop it! Georgie...

VOICE. Georgie! Wrong again!

(The spotlight is again shifted to another couple – **JOE** *and* **MISS LIPSCOMB** *– just as he steps on her toe. She winces.)*

JOE. I'm sorry if I step on your feet every once in a while. You see, I never had any dancing lessons until six months ago.

MISS LIPSCOMB. You mean to say this is not the first time you've ever danced?

JOE. N-no. I'm all right – I mean I'm better if I count to keep up with the music. I have my own way figured out.

MISS LIPSCOMB. Well, if it helps you, go ahead and count.

JOE. It's not exactly counting. I go like this: one foot, other foot, one foot, other foot, one foot, other foot...

ENSEMBLE. That's our boy!

      (The **ENSEMBLE** *points to him as they sing.)*

YOU MUST FORGIVE HIM IF HE LOOKS NEW.
HE MAY GROW OLDER – THEY OFTEN DO.
HE WEIGHS ONE HUNDRED AND FIFTY-TWO –
JOSEPH TAYLOR, JUNIOR!

      (The **ENSEMBLE** *retires.* **JOE** *is alone, gazing about him, awed.)*

JOE. I had no idea it was such a big college...sure is big.

      (Singing with assumed bravery.)

IT'S A DARN NICE CAMPUS
WITH IVY ON THE WALLS,
FRIENDLY MAPLES
OUTSIDE THE LECTURE HALLS,
A NEW GYMNASIUM,
A CHAPEL WITH A DOME –
IT'S A DARN NICE CAMPUS...
AND I WISH I WERE HOME.

      *(***CHARLIE** *enters.* **JOE** *greets him timidly.)*

Hiya, Townsend!

CHARLIE. 'Lo there, feller.

(MISS LIPSCOMB and ANOTHER COED enter and gape at CHARLIE as he passes them and exits.)

MISS LIPSCOMB. *(To the other GIRL.)* That's Charlie Townsend. Only freshman to make the Varsity.

(They turn and go past JOE.)

JOE. Good morning, Miss Lipscomb.

MISS LIPSCOMB. *(With no interest whatever.)* Hello.

(After they pass him she whispers to her COMPANION who looks back at him and giggles. They quicken their pace and exit, stifling their laughter.)

JOE. *(Pretending to himself that he hasn't noticed this.)*
IT'S A DARN NICE CAMPUS,
I'M GOING TO LIKE IT FINE!
DARN CUTE COEDS,
THEY HAVE A SNAPPY LINE;
DARN NICE FELLERS,
AS FAR AS I CAN TELL –
IT'S A DARN NICE CAMPUS...
AND I'M LONELY AS HELL!

(Cheers and applause. Lights up on:)

Scene Four:
The Football Field

(The **FRESHMEN** *are being led in the college cheer.)*

FRESHMEN. S-T-A-T-E...

(They spell it out several times, "locomotive fashion." Then a **COACH** *steps out from a* **GROUP OF PLAYERS.** *Cheers. He stops them with his uplifted hand.)*

COACH. *(Starting quietly.)* I'm just a football coach. I'm not much on making speeches... *(Sailing into it suddenly.)* But I wanna say this to you! You people up in the stands have got to do your part tomorrow. You've got to let the Wildcats know you're behind them! Yell! Yell till you're hoarse! Then yell some more. *(His voice dropping dramatically.)* This is your college – your team – *(His voice rising dramatically.)* the Wildcats!

(He points to the **TEAM,** *a tired, injured, bedraggled group of young men.)*

Don't let 'em down!

(Thunderous applause. The **CHEER LEADERS** *rushes out.)*

A CHEER LEADER. Get out your songbooks, Freshmen! Page three, *The Football Song.* Show 'em what you're goin' to do tomorrow. Hip! Hip!

[MUSIC NO. 14 "WILDCATS"]

One – two – three!

(As they start, **JOE** *is still fumbling for page three, and is a little behind the others all the way.)*

ALL.

> THE WILDCATS ARE ON A RAMPAGE!
> HEAR THOSE WILDCATS YELL – YOW!
>
>> (**JOE**, *unprepared for this shout, gives a start.*)
>
> THE WILDCATS ARE OUT TO BEAT YOU,
> TO BEAT YOU TO A FARE-THEE-WELL – WOW!
>
>> (**JOE** *is surprised again.*)
>
> WOW! WOW! WOW! GO THE WILDCATS
> AND ANOTHER TEAM GOES DOWN –
>
>> (**JOE** *puts in an extra "Wow!" here, but he is all alone. The* **CHEER LEADERS** *glare at him.*)
>
> IT'S ANOTHER DAY OF VICTORY
> FOR THE PURPLE AND BROWN!
>
>> (**JOE** *goes off in disgrace.*)

Scene Five:
The Campus

(CHARLIE enters with three gaping girls.)

CHARLIE. Did you see me in football practice? See me give that guy the old straight arm?

(Looking off, seeing JOE approach.)

Beat it girls. I've got to talk to this fellow.

(With disappointed and protesting murmurs they accept their dismissal. CHARLIE turns and greets JOE, obviously having some agenda.)

We seem to be taking the same courses. Pre-medical?

(JOE is so pleased to be addressed by the Freshman football star that if he were a dog, he would wag his tail.)

JOE. Yes. Are you?

CHARLIE. Yep. Don't know why exactly. I got an uncle in Chicago who juggles pills. Says he'll take me in with him if I'm any good.

(Getting down to the real business of the conversation.)

Say – could I have a look at your notebook?

JOE. Sure.

(He hands CHARLIE his notebook. CHARLIE looks at it.)

I've got a father who juggles pills.

(He can't help laughing as he repeats this witty and picturesque expression.)

He might take me in with him, he says.

CHARLIE. *(Whistling in admiration.)* Say! You take some notes! Don't miss a thing, do you? Would you let me borrow them?

JOE. Sure.

CHARLIE. Know what I've been reading all through the lecture? This.

> *(He takes a magazine from inside his notebook an shows it to JOE.)*

JOE. *(Reading cover.) Snappy Stories.*

CHARLIE. Ever read it? Hot stuff. I'll lend it to you.

> *(He gives it to JOE.)*

Want to come over to the house for lunch?

JOE. *(Great awe in his voice.)* House? Fraternity house?

CHARLIE. Sure. Have you been pledged to one yet?

JOE. No.

CHARLIE. I just joined one. Nice crowd. Want to come?

JOE. *(Does he want to come!)* Why, sure!

> *(They exit as the lights fade.)*

[MUSIC NO. 15 "CHANGE OF SCENE"]

Scene Six:
Jennie's Garden

(JENNIE is sitting in a swing, reading a letter sits to her friend HAZEL, who lies on the lawn, eating chocolates direct segue into:)

[MUSIC NO. 15A "JENNIE READS LETTER"]

JENNIE.
"IT'S A DARN NICE CAMPUS,
WITH IVY ON THE WALLS,
FRIENDLY MAPLES
OUTSIDE THE LECTURE HALLS.
I LIKE MY ROOMMATE
AND YOU WOULD LIKE HIM TOO –
IT'S A DARN NICE CAMPUS
BUT I'M LONELY FOR YOU."

HAZEL. That's beautiful!

(HAZEL takes a chocolate. JENNIE's father, NED BRINKER, enters.)

NED. Good evening, Hazel.

HAZEL. Hello, Mr. Brinker.

NED. *(He kisses JENNIE.)* See you got another letter from Romeo. What's in it? A lot of lovey-dovey stuff?

JENNIE. Oh, Popper! Honestly!

NED. Let's see – only two and a half more years in college – then four years in medical school – then two years as an intern – then God knows how long before he can get enough paying patients to support a wife! You're making a brilliant match, my girl. Brilliant!

JENNIE. Popper! *Honestly!*

(NED exits, chuckling.)

HAZEL. Jennie, all fooling aside, don't you ever worry about you and Joe having to wait so long?

JENNIE. 'Course I worry.

HAZEL. Why does he have to be a doctor?

JENNIE. Because his *mother* wants him to be. Her father was a doctor and her husband is a doctor, and if her darling son Joey isn't a doctor this whole town will get sick and die!

HAZEL. Gosh, I don't envy *you*! With his mother against you there isn't much you can do.

JENNIE. *(Wisely.)* Oh, I wouldn't say that, Hazel. There might be a lot I can do. Might take a little time... But I think there's a *lot* I can do.

HAZEL. Gosh, Jennie, what goes on in that little head of yours is nobody's business!

(She takes another chocolate, JENNIE smiles smugly and goes on swinging. The lights fade.)

[MUSIC NO. 16 "CHANGE OF SCENE"]

Scene Seven:
Joe's Study

(JOE sits at his desk reading a letter from JENNIE; music out.)

JENNIE'S VOICE. "Remember Hazel Skinner? She was over to see me today and I bet *your* ears burned.

(He smiles contentedly.)

"Hazel is going to marry a man named Bobby Martin. He is only one year older than you, but he is making lots of money selling automobiles.

(JOE's smile starts to fade.)

"His family wanted him to be a lawyer, but he says the trouble with professions is that you study for years and you're an old man before you make any money.

(JOE swallows hard as he turns the page.)

"I guess that's all the news. Fondly, Jennie."

(He puts the letter down on his desk and slowly takes up his Latin book and reads.)

JOE. *(Reading in meter.)* Persicos odi puer, apparatus – *(Starting to translate.)* "Odi" – I hate –

(The slam of a door is heard and CHARLIE comes into the room like a whirlwind. During the following scene he never stops doing what he came in to do – change his shirt, collar, and tie.)

CHARLIE. 'Lo, Joe.

JOE. 'Lo. What's your hurry?

CHARLIE. Late for a date. Wanna come along? I think she's got an older sister. I dunno how *much* older.

JOE. No, thanks, Charlie. I got a lot of Latin to translate.

CHARLIE. Okay, boy. You take the dead language. I'll take my live woman.

JOE. Only one I care about is back home. Just got a letter from her.

CHARLIE. Got a clean shirt?

JOE. Y-yes. But I've only got one.

CHARLIE. Swell!

(Fishing it out of a bureau drawer.)

That the dame you want to marry?

JOE. *(Looking down at JENNIE's letter.)* If she'll wait for me... I don't know if I ever told you this, Charlie, but she's the only girl I ever had a date with... I suppose you think I'm crazy.

CHARLIE. Well-ll, you're something like a guy who goes fishing for the first time in his life and decides to quit after he's caught his first fish. For all you know the waters might be filled with gorgeous and tasty tuna, and you may be settling for a sardine – I'm taking your tie. You don't mind, do you?

JOE. *(Sore.)* I'm not settling for any sardine.

(He goes back to his Latin.)

CHARLIE. 'Course you're not. She's probably a wonderful girl. Only thing I say is –

(Pointing to dollar bill on the bureau.)

Is that dollar bill yours or mine?

JOE. *(Snappily.)* Mine!

CHARLIE. *(Taking it.)* I'll pay you tomorrow when I get my check. Only thing I say is it's all right to get married eventually, but I want to have plenty of fun first.

JOE. People can have fun after they're married.

CHARLIE. What people?

JOE. My father and mother. They have lots of fun. Don't yours?

CHARLIE. I guess so. But not with each other, I don't think.

(*Putting on his coat, starting to go.*)

Sure you don't want to come? Relax?

JOE. Uh-uh.

CHARLIE. Leave that translation out so I can copy it when I get back.

JOE. (*Not looking up.*) Okay.

CHARLIE. Thanks. S'long.

JOE. So long.

(*Noticing that* **CHARLIE** *has forgotten to inch in his shirt in his trousers.*)

Hey – put my shirt in!

(*The lights fade.*)

[MUSIC NO. 17 "SCENE OF PROFESSORS"]

Scene Eight:
A Classroom

(This is a composite of all the classrooms,
FIVE PROFESSORS *stand in a large semicircle,*
each behind his own lectern, each spouting
his respective subject, in competition with
JOE's *dreams of* **JENNIE** *and the worries*
caused by her letters. **JOE** *sits at a classroom*
armchair. **CHARLIE** *sits behind him.)*

CHEMISTRY PROFESSOR. An acid is monobasic, dibasic,
or tribasic, according to the number of replaceable
hydrogen atoms.

> *(His voice drones off.)*

Thus HNO_3 is monobasic, H_2SO_4 is dibasic, H_3PO is
tribasic...

GREEK PROFESSOR. *(Overlapping his predecessor.)* ...Book
two of *The Odyssey* where we left off yesterday, Mr.
Taylor.

> *(***JOE*** does not hear because* **JENNIE** *and her*
> *last letter glide through his thoughts.)*

JENNIE. "Dear Joe: Hazel and Bob have the cutest white
stucco house. They are living together there like two
love birds. The lucky bums!"

GREEK PROFESSOR. Mr. Taylor!

> *(***JOE*** awakens and gingerly finds the place.)*

JOE. *(Rising and reading.)* "Thus did Telemachus invoke
Zeus. And the all powerful answering his prayer, sent
forth two eagles from his mountain. Swift as the wind
of a storm they flew – wing tip to wing – in lordly..."

> *(***JENNIE*** glides across stage,* **JOE**'s *lips*
> *continue to move but he is drowned out by*
> *the singing of the* **ENSEMBLE.**)*

ENSEMBLE.
>SHE IS NEVER AWAY,
>FROM HER HOME IN YOUR HEART,
>IN YOUR HEART, EVERY DAY,
>SHE IS PLAYING HER PART.

BIOLOGY PROFESSOR. All living matter proceeds from pre-existing living matter. The new form takes on the character of that from which it came.

>*(Again* **JOE***'s mind is on a new letter.)*

JENNIE. "Hazel is going to have a baby. How I envy her. That's all the news. Fondly, Jennie."

>*(***JENNIE*** glides away.)*

PHILOSOPHY PROFESSOR. The aim of philosophy is to exhibit the universe as a rational system in the harmony of its parts.

JENNIE. *(Dashing on again.)* "Dear Joe! Popper is taking me to Europe. He wants me to meet new friends!"

>*(***JENNIE*** puts on a steamer coat and a hat and runs off.)*

ENSEMBLE. New friends! Get that Joe?
>Her father wants her to find a husband –
>Some lousy nobleman perhaps!
>Where does that leave you?

CHEMISTRY PROFESSOR. A molecule is the smallest part of a substance which can exist – *alone*!

JOE. *Alone!*

ENSEMBLE. You'll never get her back
>Think of the men she'll meet on the steamer,
>And when she gets to England and Paris!

>*(***JENNIE*** enters from one side as **BERTRAM WOOLHAVEN** enters from another. They proceed to dance a passionate tango.)*

JENNIE. *(While dancing.)* I met a charming boy named Bertram Woolhaven.

ENSEMBLE. She wants to get married!
She's tired of waiting for you.

JOE. *(Very annoyed, he throws his book on the floor, and collapses in seat.)* Damn her! *Damn her!!*

JENNIE. Bertram's father is in the coal and lumber business too!

ENSEMBLE. That's the end Joe!
An alliance between two big lumber families!
It's the handwriting on the wall!

ENGLISH PROFESSOR. *(Reading Keat's "Eve of St. Agnes.")*
"Unclasps her warmed jewels one by one; Loosens her fragrant bodice;

> *(CHARLIE sits back in his seat, doing some imagining of his own. TWO GIRLS enter his dream and stand on either side of him, distrobing as Madeleine does in the poem.)*

"...By degrees
Her rich attire creeps rustling to her knees;
Half-hidden like a mermaid in seaweed,
Pensive awhile, she dreams awake, and sees
In fancy, fair St. Agnes in her bed,

> *(CHARLIE's smile has become beatific. The GIRLS stoop down and pick up their discorded clothing.)*

"But dares not look behind,
Or all the charm is led."

> *(The GIRLS drift away. One of them as she leaves his dream passes her hand lightly over CHARLIE's face and through his hair. He "awakes" with a start, rubs his face, then sits back and smiles with rapturous memory of*

the lovely vision. Now our interest reverts to
JOE.)

PHILOSOPHY PROFESSOR.   The pragmatic philosopher
searches for the hypothesis which can best serve him.

ENSEMBLE. *(To* **JOE**.*)* Philosophy, hell
You'll never drive her out of your mind!

IN YOUR HEART EVERY DAY
SHE IS PLAYING HER PART

> (**JENNIE** *enters with* **BERTRAM***; they are both
> in bathing suits.*)

JENNIE.   Bertram is teaching me to swim! We're learning
a new stroke.

> (**BERTRAM** *carries her off.*)

ENSEMBLE.
SHE IS NEVER AWAY
AND YOU'LL NEVER BE FREE!

PHILOSOPHY PROFESSOR.   The Greek philosophers finally
rebelled against fatalism. We need not be dominated,
they said –

ENSEMBLE. *(Breaking in.)* We need not submit, Joe!
We need not be dominated –
To hell with her!
Lots of good fish in the sea!

JOE. *(To* **CHARLIE** *with sudden determination.)* Did you
say that girl friend of yours had a sister?

CHARLIE.   I'll say she has!

JOE.   Then get her! I'm on the loose!

> *(He takes* **CHARLIE**'*s arm and they exit. The
> tights fade.)*

Scene Nine:
A Woodland

(CHARLIE sits on an automobile seat he has placed on the ground. A reclining female companion – MOLLY – rests her head on his lap. CHARLIE looks bored. The romance of the evening obviously has gone beyond its climax.)

CHARLIE. *(Looking at his wrist watch.)* I wonder what happened to the other two.

MOLLY. Oh, they won't get lost. My sister knows every inch of these woods. Wouldn't it be funny if she and Joe fell in love, like you and me?

CHARLIE. Yeah. Only I hope they don't take too long to fall in love. I've got an eight o'clock class.

MOLLY. Well, goodness, it was your idea to drive out here after the movie. You said it'd be romantic to sit in the woods, in the moonlight.

CHARLIE. Well, it was for a while, wasn't it?

MOLLY. Why do you say "wasn't it" like it was all over? Sometimes I think these nights don't mean to you what they mean to me. Do they?

CHARLIE. Absolutely!

(He pats her arm in an unconvincing manner.)

MOLLY. You aren't just kidding around with me, are you, Charlie?

CHARLIE. Absolutely not. What gives you ideas like that?

MOLLY. Oh, I don't know. Sometimes I think this is just a college romance. And when you graduate you'll go away and forget all about me – just like all the other boys.

CHARLIE. Like all the other boys?

MOLLY. *(After a pause while she recovers her wits.)* I mean like all the other boys with all the other girls.

CHARLIE. Let's go and look for Joe and that big sister of yours.

[MUSIC NO. 18 "CHANGE OF SCENE"]

(They rise. He picks up the automobile seat, mid they walk off.)

Scene Ten:
Another Part of the Woodland

(JOE *lies on his back.* MOLLY's *sister*, BEULAH, *looks at him ruefully.*)

BEULAH. Do you go out with girls much?

JOE. What makes you ask?

BEULAH. I was just thinking. You meet all kinds of fellows, don't you – I mean don't I?

JOE. What kind would you say I am?

BEULAH. I don't know. You're a problem.

JOE. (*With a pleased smirk.*) A problem, eh?

(*He takes out a flask.*)

Let's pep up the party.

BEULAH. Okay with me.

(*He passes her the flask.*)

Here's looking at you, Blue Eyes!

(*She passes it back to him.*)

JOE. Here's looking at you – Blue Eyes!

(*He drinks, gives the flask a shake, and hands it back to her.*)

Here, finish it up.

(*She takes it.*)

Do you know you're a hell of an attractive girl?

BEULAH. (*Passing flask back to him.*) *You* finish it up.

(*He does.*)

JOE. Beulah, what would you do if... Suppose I was the kind of a class of a type of fellow that would suddenly grab you and kiss you. What would you do?

BEULAH. But you're not that type.

JOE. No, I'm not.

BEULAH. That's what I thought.

JOE. And you're not that type of girl. You're romantic – like me.

BEULAH. Yeah...

> *(A light dawning on her.)*

Say! I'm just beginning to get you!

> *(She fluffs out her hair and proceeds to be "romantic.")*

Look at the starlight! Falling down like rain! And you and me bathing together in it – that's just an expression.

JOE. You and me, on the threshold of the unknown!

BEULAH. *(Uncertainly.)* Yeah, the unknown!

JOE. A new secret to learn, a new flower to pluck...

> *(She gives him m incredulous look.)*

A blank page to write oh!

BEULAH. Yeah, you and me both!

[MUSIC NO. 19 "SO FAR"]

NO KEEPSAKES HAVE WE
FOR DAYS THAT ARE GONE,
NO FOND RECOLLECTIONS TO LOOK BACK UPON,
NO SONG THAT WE LOVE,
NO SCENE TO RECALL –
WE HAVE NO TRADITIONS AT ALL...

WE HAVE NOTHING TO REMEMBER SO FAR, SO FAR,
SO FAR, WE HAVEN'T WALKED BY NIGHT
AND SHARED THE LIGHT OF A STAR.
SO FAR, YOUR HEART HAS NEVER FLUTTERED SO NEAR,
　　SO NEAR,
THAT MY OWN HEART ALONE COULD HEAR IT.

WE HAVEN'T GONE BEYOND THE VERY BEGINNING,
WE'VE JUST BEGUN TO KNOW HOW LUCKY WE ARE,
SO WE HAVE NOTHING TO REMEMBER, SO FAR, SO FAR –

BUT NOW I'M FACE TO FACE WITH YOU,
AND NOW AT LAST WE'VE MET
AND NOW WE CAN LOOK FORWARD TO
THE THINGS WE'LL NEVER FORGET...

> *(She puts her head on his knees. He makes up his mind to kiss her.* **JENNIE** *appears in his thoughts.)*

JENNIE. Joe!

> *(He draws away, then* **BERTRAM** *appears at* **JENNIE**'s *side.)*

Bertram!

> *(That does it.* **JOE** *kisses* **BEULAH**.*)*

BEULAH. Joe!

JOE. *(Afraid he has offended her.)* I'm sorry, Beulah. I couldn't help...

BEULAH. Joe!

> *(She throws her arms around him and kisses him with such verve that he is thrown flat on his back. Slowly he edges away from under her and, exhausted, lies prone, his head on his arm.* **BEULAH** *looks at him fondly.)*

WE HAVEN'T GONE BEYOND THE VERY BEGINNING,

WE'VE JUST BEGUN TO KNOW HOW LUCKY WE ARE,
SO WE HAVE NOTHING TO REMEMBER, SO FAR, SO FAR –

BUT NOW I'M FACE TO FACE WITH YOU,
AND NOW AT LAST WE'VE MET
AND NOW WE CAN LOOK FORWARD TO
THE THINGS WE'LL NEVER FORGET.

(Calling to him seductively.) Joe?...

> *(No answer. She leans over and looks at him
> tenderly. Then she frowns and in a voice at
> once humiliated and indignant she cries:)*

The little louse is asleep!

> *(She yanks the blanket from under him,
> throws it over her own shoulders, and stalks
> off. The lights fade as the music segues into:)*

[MUSIC NO. 20 "CHANGE OF SCENE"]

Scene Eleven:
The Campus

(JOE, walking by himself, is met by a fellow STUDENT, who hands him a letter.)

STUDENT. Letter for you, Taylor. Got mixed up with my mail.

JOE. *(Taking it.)* Thanks.

(He looks at the envelope.)

From her! *(Opening it feverishly, muttering bitterly.)* Probably announcing her engagement to Bertram! As if I cared!

CHARLIE. *(Entering, followed by GIRLS.)* Hey, Joe! I fixed up another date tonight!

JOE. *(Reading – shouting.)* She's coming home!

CHARLIE. Who?

JOE. Jennie! She's through with Bertram! Says she can't stand the sight of him! She gets home in July! Oh, how can I wait?

CHARLIE. I thought you said you were on the loose?

JOE. I'm through with that...philandering.

CHARLIE. Okay, I'll carry on for you.

JOE. *(He rejoins the GIRLS and exits.)* What'll I say when I see her? *(Frowning.)* First I'll give her a piece of my mind about this Bertram business. Shall I tell her about that girl last night? No. Let bygones be bygones. Oh, boy, July! Get away, May! Hurry up, June! Come on, you July!

(The lights fade.)

[MUSIC NO. 21 "CHANGE OF SCENE"]

Scene Twelve:
Jennie's Garden

(**JENNIE** *stands beside a bench, looking like an angel in the moonlight.* **JOE** *gazes upon her in awed rapture.*)

ENSEMBLE. There she is!
Waiting for you – the way you hoped she would be.

JENNIE. Hello, Joe.

JOE. Hello, Jennie.

ENSEMBLE. Say something wonderful to her.

JOE. I noticed your house has a new coat of paint.

JENNIE. Popper cabled ahead to have it done.

JOE. It looks nice.

ENSEMBLE. Get the conversation around to her –
To her and you!

JOE. You look different too.

JENNIE. Older?

JOE. Prettier.

ENSEMBLE. That's it! Goon!

JENNIE. Want to sit down?

JOE. Yes, I would.

ENSEMBLE. Oh, yes, yes, yes, Jennie – darling.
I want to sit next to you,
To be near you,
To touch you –

(*They sit.*)

JOE. Nice night.

JENNIE. It's just the kind of night I hoped it would be.

JOE. Did you...did you think much about tonight...too?

(**JENNIE** *nods her head.*)

JENNIE. Did you?

JOE. Quite a lot.

ENSEMBLE. You are never away from your home in my heart.

JOE. I always think of you – quite a lot.

ENSEMBLE. There is never a day...

JOE. There is never a day when you... (*Emotion coming into his voice.*) Jennie, I think about you all the time.

JENNIE. Do you Joe?

JOE. Every minute!

[MUSIC NO. 22 "YOU ARE NEVER AWAY"]

(*She nestles close to him. Timidly, he steals his arm around her.*)

JOE.	ENSEMBLE.
	HM
YOU ARE NEVER AWAY	HM
FROM YOUR HOME IN MY HEART;	HM
THERE IS NEVER A DAY	HM
WHEN YOU DON'T PLAY A PART	HM
IN A WORD THAT I SAY	HM
OR A SIGHT THAT I SEE –	HM
YOU ARE NEVER AWAY	HM
AND I'LL NEVER BE FREE.	HM HM
YOU'RE THE SMILE ON MY FACE,	
OR A SONG THAT I SING!	
YOU'RE A RAINBOW I CHASE	

JOE.   **ENSEMBLE.**

    ON A MORNING IN SPRING,

    YOU'RE A STAR IN THE LACE

    OF A WILD, WILLOW TREE –

    IN THE GREEN LEAFY LACE

    OF A WILD, WILLOW TREE.

                                       HM

    BUT TONIGHT YOU'RE NO STAR,   HM

    NOR A SONG THAT I SING;   HM

    IN MY ARMS WHERE YOU ARE

    YOU ARE SWEETER THAN SPRING;   HM

    IN MY ARMS, WHERE YOU ARE   HM

    CLINGING CLOSELY TO ME,   HM

    YOU ARE LOVELIER, BY FAR,

    THAN I DREAMED YOU COULD BE –

    YOU ARE LOVELIER MY DARLING,

    THAN I DREAMED YOU COULD BE.   HM

[MUSIC NO. 22A "YOU ARE NEVER AWAY – ENCORE"]

BASS.   **SOPRANO, ALTO & TENOR.**

    HM   AH AH AH AH

    HM   AH AH AH AH

BARITONES.

    YOU ARE NEVER AWAY

GIRLS & TENORS.

    NEVER AWAY

BARITONES.

    FROM YOUR HOME IN MY HEART;

GIRLS & TENORS.

    FROM YOUR HOME IN MY HEART;

MEN.   **WOMEN.**

    THERE IS NEVER A DAY   AH

MEN.	**WOMEN.**
WHEN YOU DON'T PLAY A PART	AH AH AH AH
AH	IN A WORD THAT I SAY
AH	OR A SIGHT THAT I SEE –

ALL.

YOU ARE NEVER AWAY
AND I'LL NEVER BE FREE.

JOE.	**ENSEMBLE.**
YOU'RE THE SMILE ON MY FACE,	AH AH
OR A SONG THAT I SING!	AH AH
YOU'RE A RAINBOW I CHASE	AH AH
ON A MORNING IN SPRING;	AH AH
YOU'RE A STAR IN THE LACE	AH AH
OF A WILD, WILLOW TREE –	AH AH
IN THE GREEN LEAFY LACE	AH AH
OF A WILD, WILLOW TREE.	AH
	AH AH AH

ENSEMBLE.

BUT TONIGHT YOU'RE NO STAR,
NOR A SONG THAT I SING;
IN MY ARMS WHERE YOU ARE
YOU ARE SWEETER THAN SPRING;

JOE.	**ENSEMBLE.**
IN MY ARMS, WHERE YOU ARE,	AH AH AH AH
CLINGING CLOSELY TO ME,	AH AH AH AH

ENSEMBLE.

YOU ARE LOVELIER, BY FAR,
THAN I DREAMED YOU COULD BE –
YOU...

JOE.

YOU ARE LOVELIER, MY DARLING,
THAN I DREAMED YOU COULD...

ALL.

BE.

[MUSIC NO. 22B "YOU ARE NEVER AWAY – EXIT"]

(He can manage only to whisper it.)

JOE. I love you.

JENNIE. I love you.

(A pause, then **JENNIE** *opens up reality.)*

Going to medical school next year?

JOE. Yep. I've been working a lot with Dad this summer. Gosh, it's exciting watching sick people get better!

JENNIE. *(Flatly.)* Is it?

JOE. You know, a doctor doesn't always know what to do at first. He tries this or that, and it doesn't do any good. Then he hits it. And you see the patient get better every day. Well then you know it's about the best thing a man can be – a doctor.

*(***JENNIE** *sits on the bench.* **JOE**, *sensing her disappointment, goes to her.)*

I'm not going to wait till I get out of medical school. We've got to get married sooner than that. I'm going to speak to my dad about it – I guess I better speak to your father too. Do you know if he likes me?

JENNIE. He likes you a lot. Only he's going to ask you about how you're going to support me.

JOE. He is?

JENNIE. The other night on the boat he was saying how he needs a young man to help him in his coal and lumber business. It's getting awful big. And now he wants to go in for farm machinery too. He might say something to you about whether you'd like to...to go in with him.

JOE. You mean instead of being a doctor?

JENNIE. Well, he'll tell you how rich we could... *(Afraid she has started this line too quickly.)* But whatever happens, Joey, it's got to be you who decides. I'd never influence one way or the other.

> *(She slides down on to* **JOE**'s *lap and nestles in his arms.)*

You have to make up your own mind – my darling.

[MUSIC NO. 23 "POOR JOE – REPRISE"]

ENSEMBLE. *(Offstage.)*
POOR JOE!
THE OLDER YOU GROW,
THE HARDER IT IS TO KNOW
WHAT TO THINK,
WHAT TO DO,
WHERE TO GO!

Scene Thirteen:
The Taylors' Porch

(**TAYLOR, MARJORIE, NED,** *and* **JENNIE** *sip lemonade and pass the time of a summer evening.*)

NED. Joe, this local hospital you're trying to build – know why you're having so much trouble raising money?

TAYLOR. Well if I...

NED. *(Breaking in.)* It's because people don't want a little hospital. They'd rather put money into a big skyscraper hospital in the nearest big town.

TAYLOR. But we need small hospitals, Ned.

MARJORIE. My father used to say he hoped the automobile would bring the patient to the doctor, instead of the doctor having to go to the patient, the way he had to do with his horse and buggy.

TAYLOR. When the snows were deep he used to have an awful time getting out to the farmer's wives when they were having their babies.

MARJORIE. That's why he built that ell on the house.

(**MARJORIE** *and* **TAYLOR** *look out front as if the ell were there.*)

TAYLOR. We put three beds in there. That was the start of our hospital. Never got any further with it. But I'm going to – when I have Joe to help me.

NED. Well, I wouldn't count on Joe too much if I were you. A young fellow like him might be too ambitious to be a small-town doctor. What do you say, Jennie?

(*There is a moment of loud silence.* **MARJORIE** *and* **TAYLOR** *exchange a look.*)

JENNIE. *(A note of warning in her voice.)* Pop, aren't you late getting started for your meeting?

NED. *(Looking at watch.)* So I am! I was due down at the Elks five minutes ago!

JENNIE. How long'll you be?

NED. Oh, not long. I'll pick you up here in about an hour. Good night, Marge. Thanks for the supper.

MARJORIE. Good night, Ned.

NED. *(As **TAYLOR** sees him out.)* Say, Joe, I got one on you. That stock I told you about has gone up twenty-two points. You were a sucker not to buy.

TAYLOR. Know what a smart man once said? If you get ten per cent on your money you can eat better.

NED. Right.

TAYLOR. And if you get two per cent on your money you can sleep better.

NED. Whoever said that didn't know much about business. Who was he?

TAYLOR. J.P. Morgan.

NED. Oh!

(He exits.)

TAYLOR. Marge, if you and Jennie'll excuse me, I'd like to go upstairs and get some reading done.

MARJORIE. Of course, Joe.

TAYLOR. Good night, Jennie.

JENNIE. Good night, Dr. Taylor.

TAYLOR. *(About to go, he turns back.)* Oh, Marge – feeling better, darling?

MARJORIE. Yes, dear.

(TAYLOR exits.)

(Who hasn't taken her eyes off JENNIE*'s face.)* What did your father mean by that, Jennie?

JENNIE. *(Innocently.)* By what, Mrs. Taylor?

MARJORIE. About Joe being too ambitious to be a small-town doctor? Has Joe said anything about that?

JENNIE. No. It's just that Pop thinks...well, he thinks it's awful for us to have to struggle along for years like... like you and Dr. Taylor.

MARJORIE. And do you agree with him?

JENNIE. Well, it seems a shame with a wonderful business like Pop's – he has no son – and he says he could teach it to Joe in a couple of years. Pop thinks Joe is smart.

MARJORIE. So do I. Joe's good at anything he likes to do. Joe's good at medicine, Jennie. His father says he's a born doctor.

JENNIE. *(Beginning to show her fangs, but sweetly.)* Oh, I don't think anybody is a born anything, do you, Mrs. Taylor?

MARJORIE. Perhaps not. But when you've watched a boy grow up, you know a lot about what...what's inside him. I don't think Joe would be happy selling coal and lumber.

JENNIE. Well I don't think I'd be happy as the wife of a starving doctor. I've got things inside of me too.

MARJORIE. I know you have, Jennie, but...

> *(Pausing, then giving the question real importance.)*

Jennie, what would you do if Joe refused to give up medicine?

JENNIE. What would I do? I'd see to it that he became a real doctor, a rich one. We'd go to some big city. I'd help him get to be the most successful doctor in town. I guess I'm more ambitious than you.

MARJORIE. Jennie, I think my husband is a very successful man. He's doing work he likes for people he likes – and he has the kind of home he needs.

JENNIE. You think I'm the wrong kind of wife for Joe, don't you?

(MARJORIE *doesn't answer.*)

Have you told him that?

MARJORIE. I haven't said a word to Joe about this. This is between you and me.

JENNIE. You don't like me and you never did – and I always knew it.

(MARJORIE *does not deny this.*)

If you're trying to get Joe away from me, all I can say is you're going to have some fight on your hands! And you may wind up by losing him altogether!

MARJORIE. I know that. But I don't think I can stand by without at least trying to save him...

JENNIE. From me?

MARJORIE. Yes.

JENNIE. When my father calls for me tell him I got tired and went home.

(*She starts off, then comes back.*)

You know, I feel better now that war's declared.

(*Pause.*)

MARJORIE. (*Coolly.*) So do I, Jennie.

JENNIE. Try and get him away from me! You just try!

> *(She exits.* **MARJORIE** *loses the outward strength she has been assuming. Thoughtfully and worried, she walks to a chair. Then suddenly she clutches it for support, her other hand going to her chest.)*

MARJORIE. *(Calling off, her voice growing progressively weaker.)* Joe – Joe, I'm out on the porch – hurry...

> *(She tries to get to the door.)*

Hurry...sweetheart...

> *(The lights fade.)*

[MUSIC NO. 24 "MARJORIE'S DEATH"]

Scene Fourteen:
Joe's Study at College

(JOE stands tense and still. CHARLIE enters. JOE passes him a telegram. CHARLIE reads it, looks at JOE with great pity and sympathy, puts his arm around him and leads him off as the lights fade.)

Scene Fifteen:
The Taylors' Porch

[MUSIC NO. 25 "INCIDENTAL (PANTOMIME)"]

(**TAYLOR** *sits beside* **MARJORIE**'s *empty chair, looking straight ahead of him, silent, grim, stunned.* **JOE** *enters, a suitcase in his hand He walks over and stands before his father. Neither can trust himself to say anything.* **TAYLOR** *looks up, smiles sadly, and motions* **JOE** *to sit in his mother's chair.* **JOE** *obeys. The two lost men sit mute, and strange with each other. Then* **JOE** *reaches over and timidly places his hand on his father's hand. The lights fade.*)

Scene Eighteen:
Outside the Church

[MUSIC NO. 26 "WHAT A LOVELY DAY FOR A WEDDING"]

(The wedding **GUESTS** *pour on.)*

GUESTS.

WHAT A LOVELY DAY FOR A WEDDING!
NOT A CLOUD TO DARKEN THE SKY.
IT'S A TREAT TO MEET AT A WEDDING,
TO LAUGH AND TO GOSSIP AND TO CRY.
WHAT A LOVELY DAY FOR A WEDDING!
WHAT A DAY FOR TWO TO BE TIED!

NED.

IT'S A LOVELY DAY FOR A WEDDING,
BUT NOT FOR THE FATHER OF THE BRIDE.

WHAT I'M ABOUT TO GET
I DON'T EXACTLY NEED –
A DOCTOR FOR A SON-IN-LAW
ANOTHER MOUTH TO FEED!

GUESTS.

WHAT HE'S ABOUT TO GET
HE DOESN'T REALLY NEED
A DOCTOR FOR A SON-IN-LAW
ANOTHER MOUTH TO FEED!

WHAT A LOVELY DAY FOR A WEDDING!
THERE'S A LIVELY TANG IN THE AIR.
IT'S A TREAT TO MEET AT A WEDDING
WHEN FAM'LIES ARE LETTING DOWN THEIR HAIR.
WHAT A LOVELY DAY FOR A WEDDING!
WE HAVE COME BY MOTOR AND SHAY.
IT'S A TREAT TO MEET AT A WEDDING
AND SAY WHAT WE USUALLY SAY.

THE TAYLOR GROUP.
> WHAT CAN HE SEE IN HER?

THE BRINKER GROUP.
> WHAT CAN SHE SEE IN HIM?

THE TAYLOR GROUP.
> THE BRINKERS ALL ARE STINKERS!

THE BRINKER GROUP.
> ALL THE TAYLOR CROWD IS GRIM!
> WHAT CAN SHE SEE IN HIM?

THE TAYLOR GROUP.
> WHAT CAN HE SEE IN HER?

ALL.
> IN MANY THINGS WE DIFFER
> BUT IN ONE THING WE CONCUR!
> IT'S A LOVELY DAY FOR A WEDDING!
> WHAT A DAY FOR TWO TO BE TIED!
> IT'S A LOVELY DAY FOR A WEDDING

NED.
> BUT NOT FOR THE FATHER OF THE BRIDE.

GIRLS.
> IT'S A LOVELY DAY FOR A WEDDING,
> NOT A CLOUD TO DARKEN THE SKY.

ALL.
> IT'S A LOVELY DAY FOR A WEDDING.

CHARLIE.
> AS LONG AS THE BRIDEGROOM ISN'T I.

GIRLS. Why?

> *(Direct segue into:)*

> **[MUSIC NO. 26A "IT MAY BE A GOOD IDEA FOR JOE"]**

CHARLIE.

> IT MAY BE A GOOD IDEA FOR JOE
> BUT WOULDN'T BE GOOD FOR ME,
> TO SIT IN A MORTGAGED BUNGALOW
> WITH MY LITTLE ONES ON MY KNEE.
> I'D MUCH RATHER GO AND BLOW MY DOUGH
> ON A CASUAL CHICKADEE.
>
> I DON'T WANT A MARK THAT I'LL HAVE TO TOW,
> MY TOE CAN GO WHERE IT WANTS TO GO.
> IT WANTS TO GO WHERE THE WILD GIRLS GROW
> IN EXTRAVAGANT QUANTITY.
>
> TO BASK IN THE WARM AND PEACEFUL GLOW
> OF CONNUBIAL CONSTANCY
> MAY BE AWFULLY GOOD FOR GOOD OLD JOE,
> BUT IT WOULDN'T BE GOOD FOR ME.

> *(Direct segue into:)*

[MUSIC NO. 27 "FINALE ACT I"]

Scene Seventeen:
Inside the Church

> (*The* **GUESTS** *are assembled The* **CHOIR**
> *marches slowly down the center aisle. The*
> **BRIDESMAIDS** *follow the* **CHOIR.** **JOE** *enters*
> *from the side,* **CHARLIE,** *his best man, behind*
> *him. They await* **JENNIE,** *who comes down*
> *the aisle on the arm of* **NED. MARJORIE,** *in*
> **JENNIE**'s *mind today, enters and stands*
> *behind* **JENNIE.**)

CHOIR.
> LET THE CHURCH LIGHT UP WITH THE GLORY
> THAT BELONGS TO EVERY BRIDE AND GROOM,
> MAY THE FIRST BRIGHT DAY OF THEIR STORY
> BE A FLOWER THAT WILL EVER BLOOM.

ENSEMBLE. (*Speaking softly.*) What happens in a church
> During the wedding march?
> What suddenly rises in our hearts, and hurts us?
> Is it the effect of the music?
> Or is it the sight of two lovers,
> Two lovers,
> Looking like two very serious children?

> (**GRANDMA** *enters* **JOE**'s *memory and stands*
> *behind him.*)

JOE. I hope I'll make Jennie a good husband.

GRANDMA. You were always a good boy.

JOE. Funny – I've been thinking a lot about Grandma
lately.

MINISTER. Dearly beloved, we are gathered together here
in the sight of God, and in the face of this company,
to join together this man and this woman in holy
matrimony.

(His lips continue to move as the **ENSEMBLE**
speak their thoughts.)

ENSEMBLE. *(Speaking softly, earnestly.)* A change has
come over us.

The simple words,

The commonplace words,

And the two serious children, listening –

A change has come over us!

The whispered jokes,

The cracks that seemed funny

A few moments ago,

Aren't funny any more!

This is no time for the humorous skeptic,

Or the gloomy prophet.

This is a time for hope.

These children desperately

Need our hope!

MINISTER. If any man can show just cause why they may
not be lawfully joined together, let him speak, or else
hereafter forever hold his peace.

(His lips continue to move as **CHARLIE,**
HAZEL, *and* **NED** *speak their thoughts.)*

CHARLIE. I hardly know the girl. She may turn out swell.

HAZEL. I know she loves him. She fought his mother, she
fought her own father. She loves him all right!

NED. The boy has a right to try medicine if he wants. He
could always come in with me later, as Jennie says.

MINISTER. Joseph, wilt thou have this woman to thy
wedded wife, to live together...

(His lips continue to move as **GRANDMA**
sings.)

GRANDMA. *(Looking at* **JOE.***)*
STARTING OUT SO FOOLISHLY SMALL,
IT'S HARD TO BELIEVE THEY WILL GROW AT ALL,
BUT WINTERS GO BY AND SUMMERS FLY,
AND ALL OF A SUDDEN THEY'RE MEN!

JOE. *(Answering the* **MINISTER.***)* I will.

MINISTER. Janet...

MARJORIE. Jennie! Listen!

MINISTER. Janet, wilt thou have, this man to thy wedded husband, to live together after God's ordinance in the holy estate of matrimony?

> *(His lips continue to move, but it is* **MARJORIE***'s insistent voice that* **JENNIE** *hears.)*

MARJORIE. Wilt thou love him, comfort him, honor, and keep him in sickness and in health; and forsaking all others, keep thee only unto him, so long as ye both shall live? Jennie?

JENNIE. *(Deeply affected.)* I will.

MINISTER. Who giveth this woman to be married to this man?

NED. I do.

MINISTER. I Joseph, take thee, Janet, to my wedded wife –

JOE. I Joseph, take thee, Janet, to my wedded wife –

MINISTER. To have and to hold from this day forward –

> *(As the* **ENSEMBLE** *sings,* **MARJORIE** *walks slowly over to* **TAYLOR** *and stands before him, as if she longed to touch him, to be alive with him for a moment.* **TAYLOR** *puts his hand to his forehead, hurt by a sudden memory.)*

ENSEMBLE.

TO HAVE AND TO HOLD
FROM THIS DAY FORWARD
FOR BETTER, FOR WORSE,
FOR RICHER, FOR POORER,
IN SICKNESS AND IN HEALTH,
TO LOVE AND TO CHERISH,
TILL DEATH DO US PART,
TILL DEATH DO US PART.

> (**CHARLIE** *steps forward and hands the ring to the* **MINISTER.**)

MINISTER. *(Placing the ring on* **JENNIE**'s *finger.)* With this ring I thee wed.

JOE. With this ring I thee wed.

> *(The* **MINISTER**'s *lips continue to move, delivering the balance of the service as the* **ENSEMBLE** *sings.)*

ENSEMBLE.

TWO MORE LOVERS
WERE MARRIED TODAY.
WISH THEM WELL!
WISH THEM WELL!
WISH THEM WELL!
BRAVE AND HAPPY,
THEY START ON THEIR WAY,
WISH THEM WELL!
WISH THEM WELL!
WISH THEM WELL!

> (**JOE** *raises* **JENNIE**'s *veil and kisses her.)*

THEY HAVE FAITH IN THE FUTURE
AND JOY IN THEIR HEARTS,
IF YOU LOOK IN THEIR EYES

YOU CAN TELL
HOW BRAVE AND HAPPY,
AND HOPEFUL ARE THEY.
WISH THEM WELL, WISH THEM WELL,
WISH THEM WELL, WISH THEM WELL,

WISH THEM WELL, WISH THEM WELL,
WISH THEM WELL, WISH THEM WELL,
WISH THEM WELL, WISH THEM WELL,
WISH THEM WELL, WISH THEM WELL,
WISH THEM WELL!

> (**JENNIE** *and* **JOE**, *married, walk up the aisle together as the* **ENSEMBLE** *sings exultantly.* **MARJORIE** *covers her eyes with her hands, afraid of what she can foresee.*)

Curtain

ACT II

[MUSIC NO. 28 "ENTR'ACTE"]

[MUSIC NO. 29 "OPENING ACT II"]

Scene One:
The Backyard of the Taylor Home

(*JENNIE in a very plain housedress, her hair in curlers, stands between a clothesline and a wash basket, a clothespin held to her mouth reflectively.* **NED** *enters carrying a garden hose and a newspaper. He walks slowly, tired and without spirit.*)

NED. Working hard, baby?

JENNIE. (*Awakened and annoyed.*) Oh...hello, Pop.

NED. Joe out making calls?

JENNIE. No, he went up to State College for a fraternity reunion.

NED. Know what I saw just now?

JENNIE. (*Resuming her work.*) No, what?

(*There is something subtly disrespectful in her voice, something that goes with* **NED** *now. He looks shabby. He has lost his bounce.*)

NED. I was passing my old place, and that fool was taking my name off! After he bought the right to use it! What do you think of that?

JENNIE. I don't know. What do *you* think of it?

NED. I think he's crazy. "Brinker's Coal and Lumber" – that's a name been known around here for years. And he puts his own name up – Ramazotti! "Ramazotti's Coal and Lumber" – what the hell does that mean?

JENNIE. It means Ramazotti owns your business.

NED. The ignorant dumbbell!

JENNIE. He also happens to own our old house. He isn't such a dumbbell.

NED. Meaning I am!

> (**JENNIE** *goes about her work in eloquent silence.*)

I'm the only one got caught in the crash, I suppose. If this government would only do something, a man'd have a chance to get back on his feet.

JENNIE. What could the government do?

NED. Well, it could do something! That's what a government is for... That Hoover!

MILLIE. *(Offstage.)* Jennie...

JENNIE. Hello, Millie.

MILLIE. *(Offstage.)* Come on over and see the chinchilla coat.

JENNIE. I've got to hang my wash. You and the girls come over here.

MILLIE. *(Offstage.)* All right.

NED. Who's got a chinchilla coat?

JENNIE. Nobody. It's a picture of one in *Vogue*.

NED. I was going to say! What woman can afford expensive furs these days?

JENNIE. Lots of women – Mrs. Ramazotti, for instance.

NED. You're always throwing that up to me. Damn it! Everybody's poor these days. You're lucky your husband is a professional man who makes a decent living. Gives you a roof over your head.

JENNIE. He gives you a roof over *your* head too.

NED. *(Hurt.)* It's...all in the family, isn't it?

> *(He exits.)*

JENNIE. I'm sorry. *(Muttering to herself as she works.)* Decent living! If I thought that was all we'd ever have, I'd just as soon die!

> *(HAZEL enters with ADDIE.)*

HAZEL. Here it is.

> *(She hands the magazine to JENNIE, who gazes at the turned page, dumbfounded MILLIE and DOT enter. All the girls wear cheap print dresses, young housewives like JENNIE, and as poor.)*

ADDIE. Isn't that the dreamiest coat you ever saw?

MILLIE. Terrific!

JENNIE. To think some girls actually get things like this!

HAZEL. And they're the kind who don't do any housework.

DOT. All they do is try to look beautiful.

HAZEL. And men think they're wonderful.

MILLIE. *(Laughing.)* Look. On the opposite page is an article – "Money Isn't Everything."

JENNIE. Well, fine. I don't want everything. I'll just take money.

> **[MUSIC NO. 30 "MONEY ISN'T EVERYTHING"]**

MILLIE. *(Reading from magazine.)*
"MONEY ISN'T EVERYTHING!
WHAT CAN MONEY BUY?"

OTHER FOUR GIRLS.
AN AUTOMOBILE, SO YOU WON'T GET WET –
CHAMPAGNE, SO YOU WON'T GET DRY!

MILLIE. *(Reading.)*
"MONEY ISN'T EVERYTHING!
WHAT HAVE RICH FOLKS GOT?"

OTHER FOUR GIRLS.
A FLORIDA HOME, SO YOU WON'T GET COLD –
A YACHT SO YOU WON'T GET HOT!

DOT.
AN ORCHID OR TWO
SO YOU WON'T FEEL BLUE
IF YOU HAVE TO GO OUT AT NIGHT.

ADDIE.
AND MAYBE A JAR
OF CAVIAR
SO YOUR APPETITE WON'T BE LIGHT!

MILLIE. *(Reading.)*
"OIL TYCOON AND CATTLE KING,
RADIO TROUBADOUR,
BELITTLE THE FUN THAT THEIR FORTUNES BRING,
AND TELL YOU THAT THEY ARE SURE
MONEY ISN'T EVERYTHING!"

ALL GIRLS.
MONEY ISN'T EVERYTHING,
MONEY ISN'T EVERYTHING –

JENNIE & HAZEL.
UNLESS YOU'RE POOR!

MILLIE. It says here –

(Reading.)

"CAN MONEY MAKE YOU HONEST?
CAN IT TEACH YOU RIGHT FROM WRONG?
CAN MONEY KEEP YOU HEALTHY?
CAN IT MAKE YOUR MUSCLES STRONG?"

ADDIE.

CAN MONEY MAKE YOUR EYES GET RED,
THE WAY THEY DO FROM SEWING?
CAN MONEY MAKE YOUR BACK GET SORE,
THE WAY IT GETS FROM MOWING?

DOT.

CAN MONEY MAKE YOUR HANDS GET ROUGH,
AS WASHING DISHES DOES?

JENNIE & HAZEL.

CAN MONEY MAKE YOU SMELL THE WAY
THAT COOKING FISHES DOES?

MILLIE.

"IT MAY BUY YOU GEMS AND FANCY CLOTHES
AND JUICY STEAKS TO CARVE,
BUT IT CANNOT BUILD YOUR CHARACTER –"

ADDIE & DOT.

OR TEACH YOU HOW TO STARVE!

MILLIE.

"MONEY ISN'T EVERYTHING!
IF YOU'RE RICH, YOU PAY –"

ADDIE & DOT.

ELIZABETH ARDEN TO DO YOUR FACE
THE NIGHT YOU ATTEND A PLAY!

ADDIE, DOT & MILLIE. *(Singing dreamily, while* **JENNIE**
and **HAZEL** *pantomime the thrilling event.)*

FEELING LIKE THE BLOOM OF SPRING,
DOWN THE AISLE YOU FLOAT!

A TIFFANY RING, AND A CARTIER STRING
OF PEARLS TO ADORN YOUR THROAT!
YOUR CARNEGIE DRESS
WILL BE MORE OR LESS
OF A HANDKERCHIEF ROUND YOUR HIP,
SEWED ON TO YOU SO
THAT YOUR SLIP WON'T SHOW –

JENNIE & HAZEL.

AND WHATEVER YOU SHOW WON'T SLIP!

ADDIE, DOT & MILLIE.

TO YOUR CREAMY SHOULDERS CLING
ERMINES WHITE AS SNOW.
THEN ON TO CAFES WHERE THEY SWAY AND SWING
YOU GO WITH YOUR WEALTHY BEAU.
THERE YOU'LL HEAR A CROONER SING –

ALL. *(Imitating Rudy Vallee.)*
"MONEY ISN'T EVERYTHING!"

(As themselves.)

MONEY ISN'T EVERYTHING,
AS LONG AS YOU HAVE DOUGH!

(Direct segue into:)

[MUSIC NO. 31 "DANCE"]

*(**HAZEL** dances to depict the life of an idly rich and self-centered woman. The lights fade.)*

[MUSIC NO. 32 "CHANGE OF SCENE"]

Scene Two:
Joe and Jennie's Bedroom

(JENNIE *sits up in bed glaring at* JOE, *who stands before her.*)

JENNIE. (*Extreme irritation in her voice.*) This isn't true. You're trying to be funny.

JOE. No, I'm not Charlie's uncle came to the reunion especially to talk to me.

JENNIE. And you were offered a chance to be his partner? A partner of Dr. Denby?

JOE. Well, you see, I was a kind of a white-haired boy of Denby's when I was an intern at his hospital, and...

JENNIE. And you have the nerve to stand there and tell me you turned him down! Turned down a partnership in his office and...

JOE. I've got to think of my father. I'm just beginning to be some help to him.

JENNIE. What it gets down to is this – you care more about your father than you do about me.

JOE. (*Out of patience.*) It's got nothing to do with caring about anybody. I'm just not going to walk out on my father. For you, or Charlie, or anybody. I'm not going to do it, that's all!

(*He exits; a door slams; silence.* JENNIE *puffs at her cigarette thoughtfully.*)

ENSEMBLE WOMEN. Go easy, Jennie!
When a man slams a bathroom door like that;
You're in trouble!
Use your head!
This is the biggest chance you'll ever have –
Maybe the *only* chance –

To get the kind of life you want.

Don't throw it away with a few angry words.

Use your head.

This is the most important night of your life!

> (**JOE** *enters, his coat off and his tie loosened.*
> *He sits in a chair.*)

Be clever!

> (**JENNIE** *looks over at him and sniffles softly,*
> *then looks away.* **JOE** *doesn't react; she sniffles*
> *louder. Still no reaction from* **JOE**.)

He must have heard you.

Lord knows, you sniffed loud enough.

He didn't even ask what you were crying about.

That's bad!

Better do something

Or say something – quick

JENNIE. *(Sniffling a childish little sob.)* Have you got a hanky?

> (**JOE** *gives her his handkerchief.*)

Thankee!

> (*She looks up sidewise to see if he grins. No*
> *grin.*)

ENSEMBLE. There's a wall between you.

You'll have to do something more...

Well...radical!

Don't you think you'd better...

Sort of...

Go to him?

> (**JENNIE** *immediately rises, throws a robe over*
> *her nightgown without wrapping it around*

her, and patters in her bare feet over to **JOE.**
She slips down on to his lap, puts her arms
around him, buries her head in his chest, and
sobs. He is touched; he holds her tighter.)

JOE. Don't cry, Jennie. Nothing to cry about.

JENNIE. I'm a mean, selfish girl! I wasn't thinking of you.
I was only thinking of myself and how wonderful it
would be to have a beautiful house in Chicago, and
servants, and lovely dresses to wear so I could look
pretty for you when you came home at night.

ENSEMBLE. Good!

(They retire.)

JOE. I know how tough it's been for you, Jennie. Gosh,
cooking three meals a day is bad enough, without the
rest of the housework.

JENNIE. Three meals for four people – that's twelve meals
a day, you silly!

JOE. I wish I could explain just how I feel about this
Chicago thing. It's... I don't know...

JENNIE. *(Rising.)* Don't worry about it, darling – you're a
better judge of what you can do than I am.

JOE. What do you mean?

JENNIE. Well, I suppose you're worried about whether you
could handle a big city practice.

JOE. Me? Oh, I could handle it all right! Why do you
suppose they want me?

JENNIE. *(Craftily.)* Well, I... Goodness! *I* think you're the
best doctor in the world. Only it looked to me as if you
might be afraid to tackle...

JOE. Afraid! Of course not! I just feel... if I *did* want to go,
I don't know how I could ever break it to Dad. Don't
know how I could even open up the subject.

(**JENNIE** *chuckles.*)

What're you laughing at?

JENNIE. The way my mind rushes on when I get excited. When you told me about this, I thought of a million things all at once! First thing I thought of was we'd soon be so rich you could give your father that old ten thousand dollars he needs to complete the hospital.

> (**JOE** *looks thoughtful, and* **JENNIE** *is quick to follow with another ace.*)

Know what else I was thinking? I was thinking now at last we could afford something – something I've wanted ever since we were married – even before we were married. He'd be – or she'd be – the most important thing in my life, next to you.

> (*She patters over to him, kneels at his feet, and presses her head to his knee in pretty shyness.*)

[MUSIC NO. 33 "POOR JOE – REPRISE"]

ENSEMBLE MEN. *(Offstage.)*
POOR JOE!
THE OLDER YOU GROW,
THE HARDER IT IS TO KNOW
WHAT TO THINK,
WHAT TO DO,
WHERE TO GO!

JENNIE. I'm home alone so much... I have a lot of time to think and dream. You're so busy, you don't have a chance.

JOE. Oh, yes, I do. What do you suppose I think of all day, in between calls, driving from one house to the other?

JENNIE. What?

JOE. Same girl I've been thinking about since I was eight
   years old.

[MUSIC NO. 34 "CHANGE OF SCENE (YOU ARE NEVER AWAY – REPRISE)"]

YOU'RE THE SMILE ON MY FACE,
OR A SONG THAT I SING!
YOU'RE A RAINBOW I CHASE
ON A MORNING IN SPRING;
YOU'RE A STAR IN THE LACE
OF A WILD, WILLOW TREE –
IN THE GREEN LEAFY LACE
OF A WILD, WILLOW TREE.

BUT TONIGHT YOU'RE NO STAR,
NOR A SONG THAT I SING;
IN MY ARMS WHERE YOU ARE

YOU ARE SWEETER THAN SPRING;
IN MY ARMS, WHERE YOU ARE,
CLINGING CLOSELY TO ME,
YOU ARE LOVELIER, BY FAR,
THAN I DREAMED YOU COULD BE –
YOU ARE LOVELIER, MY DARLING,
THAN I DREAMED YOU COULD BE.

> (**JENNIE** *looks up at him and blinks her eyes
> like a little child.*)

JENNIE. Baby's sleepy.

> (**JOE** *kisses her, picks her up, and starts to
> carry her back to the bed.*)

ENSEMBLE MEN. *(Offstage.)* That's all, brother!

> (*The lights fade.*)

[MUSIC NO. 35 "CHANGE OF SCENE"]

Scene Three:
Dr. Taylor's Office

> (**TAYLOR** *stands looking at two diplomas that hang side by side – his own and Joe's.*)

JOE. *(Offstage.)* Dad?...

> (**TAYLOR** *gingerly slips back to his desk, not wanting* **JOE** *to come in and find him looking at the diplomas.*)

...Dad?...

> (**JOE** *enters.*)

TAYLOR.   Hello, Joe. Just looking over your parting instruction.

JOE. *(Tactfully.)* Not instructions, Dad. Just a few...er... suggestions about the people I've been taking care of. I particularly wanted to talk about that Reilly kid.

> *(He points over his father's shoulder to the top page of notes.)*

TAYLOR. *(Looking down at it.)* Oh, I know Vincent. Works on the farm all day and studies all night. Wants to be a priest.

JOE. That's the one.

TAYLOR. Put on any weight?

> (**JOE** *shakes his head.*)

What are you doing for him?

JOE. Well, yesterday I called in a vet. I had him take a look at the Reilly's cow.

> *(A pause as **TAYLOR** looks at **JOE**.)*

TAYLOR. T.B.?

(**JOE** *nods.*)

Well, if Vincent's tubercular I'll call up the commissioner and get him put on the list for the state sanitarium.

JOE. That'll mean giving up his studies, won't it?

TAYLOR. 'Course it will. He oughtn't to do anything for a couple of years.

JOE. Well you see that's our biggest worry, Dad. He's going to think he'll be too old to go back to his studies. The only reason he wants to live is to be a priest. We've got to...you've got to see that he doesn't lose hope.

TAYLOR. (*Looking at* **JOE** *with an understanding smile.*) Well, I'll do what I can, Joe.

(*He picks up another paper.*)

Jan Malinowski – the old Polish fellow with a chronic catarrh?

JOE. Well, the only note I made about him is that I haven't been charging him anything.

TAYLOR. We'll continue that policy.

JOE. He's out of work now.

TAYLOR. (*Studying* **JOE**.) Get kind of wrapped up in these people don't you?

JOE. (*Self-consciously.*) Yes...you do...don't you?

TAYLOR. One night – I was about fourteen I guess – I was out in the barn hitching the mare to your grandfather's sleigh. He had a bad chest cold – probably running a fever – but he was going to drive twelve miles through a blizzard on a call. I asked him why – asked him if it was because he loved people so much. He said, "Hell no!" Didn't give a hoot about them – didn't really like anybody till after he had done something for them. After that he figured he had a stake in them.

JOE. I see what he meant.

(**MARJORIE** *enters.*)

MARJORIE. Of course you do. They're your people after you've helped them.

(*Coming up close behind* **JOE**.)

Why does your heart feel so heavy?
If it is so fine to go to Chicago –
To be rich and successful and famous –
Why does your heart feel heavy?
You could still change your mind!
Let the train go without you!

(*Sound of an auto horn.*)

TAYLOR. I guess that's Jennie in the car.

MARJORIE. Lean out the window and tell her it's all off.

(**JOE** *starts for window.* **CHARLIE***'s face appears before him, dimly lit.*)

CHARLIE. You going nuts? People will think you are crazy. Not just Jennie. Me. Everybody.

(**CHARLIE** *disappears.* **JOE** *turns back from the window.*)

TAYLOR. (*Holding out his hand.*) Well... Good luck, son.

JOE. (*Blurting it all out.*) I'm doing this for Jennie, Father. It'll be easier for her, and it's a wonderful practice – wonderful people. I even figured in a few years I might be able to give you the ten grand you need to finish the hospital.

TAYLOR. Fine, Joe! Just fine!

JOE. And another thing. Now, Jennie and I can afford to have a baby.

MARJORIE. Your father and I didn't know whether we could afford you or not. We just wanted you.

> (*Again the automobile horn offstage.*)

JOE. Well...so long, Dad.

> (*He turns to go, then suddenly stops and wheels around.* **MARJORIE** *and* **TAYLOR** *stand transfixed with wild hope.*)

I forgot my diploma.

[MUSIC NO. 36 "INCIDENTAL (A FELLOW NEEDS A GIRL – REPRISE)"]

> (**JOE** *crosses and takes down his diploma.* **MARJORIE** *goes to* **TAYLOR**, *throws her arms around him from behind and holds both hands on his heart.*)

MARJORLE. You're hurt!

JOE. Guess I can get this in the big suitcase.

MARJORIE. I'm here with you darling,
I love you.
Don't let him hurt you.

TAYLOR. (*His voice is hoarse as he attempts to throw the thing off lightly.*) Lucky you remembered that. A doc isn't much good with out his shingle. They'd think you were a horse doctor or something. No room for horse doctors in a fancy office like that.

> (**JOE** *and* **TAYLOR** *force a laugh.* **JOE** *gulps and fearing to trust his voice further, waves at his father as he starts out* **TAYLOR** *calls to him, a tired smile on his face.*)

Don't take any wooden nickels.

> (**JOE** *is gone.* **TAYLOR** *sinks down at his desk.*)

MARJORIE.
    A FELLOW NEEDS A GIRL
    TO SIT BY HIS SIDE
    AT THE END OF A WEARY DAY,
    TO SIT BY HIS SIDE
    AND LISTEN TO HIM TALK
    AND AGREE WITH THE THINGS HE'LL SAY.

        *(**TAYLOR***'s head falls to his arms as the lights*
        fade. Direct segue into:)

        [MUSIC NO. 37 "YATATA, YATATA, YATATA"]

Scene Four:
Joe and Jennie's Apartment in Chicago

(A mass of **CHATTERING PEOPLE** *packed close together.* **JARMAN,** *a butler, and a* **MAID** *carrying drinks hold their trays aloft so they can worm in and out of the crowd.* **JENNIE** *glides from one guest to another with the manner of an assured hostess.)*

ALL.
YA-TA-TA, YA-TA-TA, YA-TA-TA, YA-TA-TA
YA-TA-TA, YA-TA-TA, YA-TA-TA, YA-TA-TA

WOMAN. *(To another* **WOMAN,** *with great expression.)*
BROCCOLI!

MAN. *(Answering in the same gushing manner.)*
HOGWASH!

ANOTHER MAN. *(To* **WOMAN.)**
BALDERDASH!
(To **ANOTHER WOMAN.)** PHONEY BALONEY!

WOMAN. *(Answering.)*
TRIPE AND TRASH!

ALL.
YA-TA-TA, YA-TA-TA, YA-TA-TA, YA-TA-TA
YA-TA-TA, YA-TA-TA, YA-TA-TA, YA-TA-TA

WOMAN. *(To* **TWO OTHER WOMEN.)**
BUSY! BUSY! I'M BUSY AS A BEE!
I START THE DAY AT HALF PAST ONE!
WHEN I AM FINISHED PHONING
IT'S TIME TO DRESS FOR TEA.

ALL THREE WOMEN.
NOTHING WE HAVE TO DO GETS DONE!

CHARLIE. *(To himself, reflectively.)*
THE DEEP-THINKING GENTLEMEN AND LADIES
WHO KEEP A METROPOLIS ALIVE,
DRINK COCKTAILS
AND KNOCK TAILS

> *(Which they all do in two beats.)*

EV'RY AFTERNOON AT FIVE.

> *(To a new arrival – **DR. BIGBY DENBY** – a distinguished-looking gentleman with white hair.)*

Hello, Uncle!

ALL.
YA-TA-TA, YA-TA-TA, YA-TA-TA, YA-TA-TA
YA-TA-TA, YA-TA-TA, YA-TA-TA, YA-TA-TA

MAN. *(To **WOMAN**, indicating the new arrival.)*
THERE GOES DOCTOR DENBY!

ANOTHER MAN. *(To his companion.)*
DOCTOR BIGBY DENBY!

ALL.
BIGBY DENBY, BIGBY DENBY, BIGBY DENBY, BIGBY DENBY!

THREE WOMEN. *(Surrounding **DENBY**.)*
DOCTOR! DOCTOR!
I NEED ANOTHER SHOT!

FOUR OTHER WOMEN. *(Explaining to a **THIRD GROUP**.)*
THE SHOTS HE GIVES ARE TOO DIVINE!

ONE WOMAN.
HE FILLS A LITTLE NEEDLE AND HE GIVES YOU ALL IT'S GOT!

ANOTHER WOMAN.
YOUR FANNY HURTS BUT YOU FEEL FINE!

ALL.

> YA-TA-TA, YA-TA-TA, YA-TA-TA
> BROCCOLI, HOGWASH, BALDERDASH,
> YA-TA-TA, YA-TA-TA, YA-TA-TA
> YA-TA-TA, YA-TA-TA, YA-TA-TA
> PHONEY BALONEY, TRIPE AND TRASH!
> YA-TA-TA, YA-TA-TA, YA-TA-TA, YA-TA-TA
> YA-TA-TA, YA-TA-TA, YA-TA-TA, YA-TA-TA
> GOODNESS KNOWS WHERE THE DAY HAS GONE!
> THE DAYS COME FAST AND ARE QUICKLY GONE,
> BUT THE TALK, TALK, TALK GOES ON AND ON
> AND ON AND ON AND ON!

FOUR MEN. *(Indicating* **LANSDALE**, *who is telling a story to a sycophantic group that includes* **JENNIE**.*)*

> LANSDALE! LANSDALE!
> THE MULTIMILLIONAIRE!
> HE MANUFACTURES LANSDALE SOAP!

CHARLIE.

> SO WHEN HE TELLS A STORY
> HIS LISTENERS DECLARE,
> "HE'S TWICE AS COMICAL AS BOB HOPE!"

> > *(***LANSDALE***'s listeners smack their thighs and bend over as they laugh.)*

ALL.

> YA-TA-TA, YA-TA-TA, YA-TA-TA, YA-TA-TA
> YA-TA-TA, YA-TA-TA, YA-TA-TA, YA-TA-TA...

> > *(The* **ENSEMBLE** *continues softly underneath dialogue.)*

MRS. LANSDALE. *(Shouting right in the face of a* **FRIEND**.*)* I can't sleep at night!

MAN. *(To a sympathetic* **YOUNG WOMAN**.*)* When I was four years old I tried to murder my nurse. My psychiatrist says my wife is taking her place.

DENBY. *(To an extremely* **HEALTHY LOOKING WOMAN.***)* What you need little lady is a good rest! One month at Hot Springs for you! Golf, dancing!

HEALTHY WOMAN. Oh, thank you, doctor!

DENBY. And when you come back I'll give you some shots.

(He gives her an assuring pat on the shoulder and a pinch on the cheek.)

MRS. LANSDALE. *(Telling it to* **SOMEONE ELSE.***)* Not one wink!

CHARLIE. *(To a* **PATIENT.***)* Hot Springs for you, little lady.

PATIENT. I just came from Hot Springs.

CHARLIE. All right then, Palm Springs!

(He gives her the same pat and pinch that his uncle gave his **PATIENT.** **NED** *appears in the crowd, well dressed and with his old assurance returned.)*

NED. *(To* **LANSDALE.***)* If the government would only let us alone – that Roosevelt!

MRS. LANSDALE. *(Yelling at* **ANOTHER FRIEND.***)* I've tried reading a book!

WOMAN. *(Pointing across the room.)* Look at Mrs. Mulhouse! She simply doesn't know how to drink!

*(***MRS. MULHOUSE** *has the goofy, faraway look of someone about to pass out.)*

JENNIE. Jarman!

*(***JARMAN** *passes his tray to* **JENNIE,** *hoists* **MRS. MULHOUSE** *over his shoulder as if this were all a part of his normal routine, and starts out with her.)*

CHARLIE. *(To himself.)*
   THE DEEP THINKING GENTLEMEN AND LADIES
   WHO KEEP A METROPOLIS ALIVE,
   DRINK COCKTAILS
   AND KNOCK TAILS
   EV'RY AFTERNOON AT FIVE.

ALL.
   YA-TA-TA, YA-TA-TA, YA-TA-TA, YA-TA-TA
   YA-TA-TA, YA-TA-TA, YA-TA-TA, YA-TA-TA...

   (The **ENSEMBLE** *continues softly under dialogue.)*

NED. *(To a* **MAN.***)* All I ever see those WPA guys do is lean on their shovels.

LANSDALE. *(To a* **WOMAN,** *finishing a story with an impressive gesture.)* And I sank a ten-foot putt.

   *(***JOE** *appears, carrying a tray of cocktails, looking as silly as he feels. He passes them to the* **MAID,** *but* **JENNIE** *comes along immediately with a fresh tray, which she presses into* **JOE***'s hands, pantomiming instruction as to where he must go with it. He starts off but is quickly intercepted by the sleepless* **MRS. LANSDALE.***)*

MRS. LANSDALE. Barbital, membutal, luminal, tuinal... *(With a helpless gesture.)* Wide awake!

JOE. *(His manner just like* **DENBY***'s and* **CHARLIE***'s.)* Little lady, my advice to you is a good long rest. Lake Louise, Canada! The smell of the pines will put you to sleep.

MRS. LANSDALE. *(She'll be damned if anything is going to put her to sleep!)* Suppose it doesn't?

JOE. Then come home and we'll try giving you some...

ALL. *(Breaking in.)*
>BROCCOLI, HOGWASH, BALDERDASH,
>PHONEY BALONEY, TRIPE AND TRASH.

DENBY.
>GOODNESS KNOWS WHERE THE YEARS HAVE GONE!

ALL.
>THE YEARS OF A LIFE ARE QUICKLY GONE,
>BUT THE TALK, TALK, TALK GOES ON AND ON,
>GOES ON AND ON AND ON.
>
>The prattle and the tattle,
>The gab and the gush,
>The chatter and the patter
>And the twaddle and the tush
>Go on and on and on and on and...
>
>YA-TA-TA, YA-TA-TA, YA-TA-TA, YA-TA-TA
>YA-TA-TA, YA-TA-TA, YA-TA-TA, YA-TA-TA...

>>*(They continue, their voices fading as the lights fade out.)*

Scene Five:
The Foyer of the Taylor Apartment

(**EMILY,** *a neatly dressed young woman, is discovered seated at small table. She has a briefcase on her lap.* **JARMAN** *crosses with* **MRS. MULHOUSE** *over his shoulder.*)

EMILY. Good evening, Jarman. Is that Mrs. Mulhouse you've got there?

JARMAN. *(Laconically.)* Yes.

(*He exits.*)

JOE. *(Entering with a highball in his hand.)* Hello, Emily. What's on your mind?

EMILY. *(Taking an X-ray film from her brief case.)* I won't keep you long.

JOE. I brought along a drink for you.

EMILY. Thanks, doctor, I don't feel like one just now.

JOE. *(Putting the drink on the table.)* What have you got there?

EMILY. X-ray films. Gilbert Martin's.

JOE. *(In a tone of mild rebuke.)* But I've already looked at them. You were there, Emily. Don't you remember? I told you to phone him and tell him there was nothing to worry about.

EMILY. I remember.

JOE. Did you phone him?

EMILY. Nn-no.

JOE. *(Irritated.)* Why not?

EMILY. After you left I took a squint at it.

(*Handing him the X-ray films.*)

JOE. Think the aging doctor's eyes are going back on him, eh?

> *(He holds the films up to the lamplight.)*

EMILY. You were in such a hurry to leave this afternoon! Don't blame you of course, with fifty guests here – all high-bracket patients, and hospital trustees...

> *(**JOE** gives her a quick look, not sure if she is ribbing him or not. She dodges that issue by getting back to the film.)*

See what I mean, doctor?

> *(She points to a spot on the film.)*

Couldn't that be an ulcer crater?

JENNIE. *(Entering.)* Darling! You must come inside! Mrs. Lansdale is just leaving and she wants to talk to you. *(To **EMILY**, impressively.)* Mrs. Brook Lansdale.

EMILY. I know. Twenty million dollars and she can't sleep.

JENNIE. She wants to talk to my husband about donating three hundred thousand dollars toward our new private pavilion. *(To **JOE**, whose eyes have not left the X-ray film.)* I guess that's about as important to you as anything else can be right now, isn't it, Joe?

> *(She gives **EMILY** a sharp look.)*

I'll go right in to her.

EMILY. Shall I phone Mr. Martin and tell him that his stomach is fine and dandy?

> *(**JOE** is now pretty sure he was wrong about the X-ray, but he hasn't quite got around to admitting it.)*

JOE. Er...no. I'd like to look at it in the office. I don't trust this light.

JENNIE. Hurry, Joe! She'll be gone! I'll stay here and talk to Miss West.

EMILY. I'm just going.

JOE. Good night, Emily.

EMILY. Good night, doctor.

JOE. And thanks for calling this to my attention. It was nice of you to come all the way up in this kind of weather.

JENNIE. Joe! Don't dawdle! She'll be gone!

JOE. All right, dear, all right!

> *(He exits.)*

JENNIE. Forgive me for taking him away from you. Social contacts play such an important part in a practice like ours.

EMILY. Half the battle.

JENNIE. Exactly.

EMILY. A big medical practice is like any other big business. If you want to be an important doctor with important patients, you've got to give time to them, play golf with them, go to their homes for dinner, have them to your house for cocktails.

> *(She makes a gesture that indicates the present party. JENNIE smiles and nods her agreement.)*

Of course you haven't got time to do that with every stumblebum who gets sick, so you concentrate on the big ones –

> *(JENNIE knits her brows, not quite sure of EMILY.)*

The leaders of the community!

JENNIE. That's just what I tell the doctor – just the phrase
I use! The leaders of the community!

EMILY. You're so right, Mrs. Taylor!

JENNIE. Of course I'm not criticizing my husband, but he
isn't the most practical man in the world.

EMILY. Kind of a softy.

JENNIE. That's right. And he's inclined to give too *much*
time to the little things and not enough to the things
that count.

EMILY. Oh, I think he's learning, Mrs. Taylor... He's
learning fast.

JENNIE. *(Picking up* EMILY*'s drink from the table where*
JOE *left it.)* He left his drink. I'll take it to him.

EMILY. *(With sudden, impulsive bluntness.)* That's mine!

JENNIE. Oh – sorry.

EMILY. *(Taking it from her.)* Thank you.

> *(She finishes the drink in one swallow and
> hands the empty glass back to* JENNIE.*)*

Good night!

> *(And she leaves the astonished* JENNIE *as the
> lights fade.)*

[MUSIC NO. 37A "CHANGE OF SCENE"]

Scene Six:
The Street Entrance to the Apartment Building

(TWO COUPLES and a uniformed DOORMAN stand in the rain. The DOORMAN blows a whistle several times. EMILY enters and after waiting a few seconds, addresses him.)

EMILY. Are all these people ahead of me?

DOORMAN. They are, Miss.

EMILY. I'll go around to the avenue and take my chances.

DOORMAN. Please yourself.

(He didn't expect much of a tip from her anyway. He leads the others off to a taxi. EMILY walks in the other direction. Her eyes follow an imaginary cab as it whizzes by. She puts her collar up.)

EMILY. Taxi – taxi... *(Mumbling to herself.)* This is what I get for being a Girl Scout. Save the doc, save the patient, and get pneumonia myself. Way I feel now, I wouldn't care much. That wife of his leads him around by the nose. Well –

[MUSIC NO. 38 "THE GENTLEMAN IS A DOPE"]

If a man lets himself be led by the nose, that's all he rates!

THE BOSS GETS ON MY NERVES,
I'VE GOT A GOOD MIND TO QUIT.
I'VE TAKEN ALL I CAN,
IT'S TIME TO GET UP AND GIT
AND MOVE TO ANOTHER JOB,
OR MAYBE ANOTHER TOWN!
THE GENTLEMAN BURNS ME UP!

THE GENTLEMAN GETS ME DOWN.

THE GENTLEMAN IS A DOPE,
A MAN OF MANY FAULTS,
A CLUMSY JOE WHO WOULDN'T KNOW
A RHUMBA FROM A WALTZ.
THE GENTLEMAN IS A DOPE,
AND NOT MY CUP OF TEA –
WHY DO I GET IN A DITHER?
HE DOESN'T BELONG TO ME!

THE GENTLEMAN ISN'T BRIGHT,
HE DOESN'T KNOW THE SCORE –
A CAKE WILL COME, HE'LL TAKE A CRUMB
AND NEVER ASK FOR MORE.
THE GENTLEMAN'S EYES ARE BLUE,
BUT LITTLE DO THEY SEE –
WHY AM I BEATING MY BRAINS OUT?
HE DOESN'T BELONG TO ME!

HE'S SOMEBODY'S ELSE'S PROBLEM,
SHE'S WELCOME TO THE GUY!
SHE'LL NEVER UNDERSTAND HIM
HALF AS WELL AS I.

THE GENTLEMAN IS A DOPE,
HE ISN'T VERY SMART.
HE'S JUST A LUG YOU'D LIKE TO HUG
AND HOLD AGAINST YOUR HEART.
THE GENTLEMAN DOESN'T KNOW
HOW HAPPY HE COULD BE –
LOOK AT ME CRYTNG MY EYES OUT
AS IF HE BELONGED TO ME!
HE'LL NEVER BELONG TO ME.

(She resumes searching the streets for a cab.)

Hey, taxi...

THE GENTLEMAN IS A DOPE...

Taxi!

THE GENTLEMAN IS A DOPE...

Hey, ta... Oh, hell, I'll walk!

(She digs her hands into her raincoat pockets and stamps off as the lights fade.)

[MUSIC NO. 39 "CHANGE OF SCENE"]

Scene Seven:
Dr. Denby's Private Office

(DENBY is alone in his office; JOE enters.)

JOE. You sent for me, doctor?

DENBY. Oh, yes, come in. Sit down, doctor. Two things. First about yourself. I am very pleased with you, Joseph. Not only because of your work here at the office, but at the hospital. You...well you have won the regard of Brook Lansdale and the approval of our – ha! ha! – biggest trustee is even more important than *my* approval, hmm? *(Changing quickly.)* Now I come to my second topic – Charlie, my nephew. In this recent... ah...rebellion at the hospital – the nurses demanding eight-hour duty – he actually took their side! You don't think he's been drinking too much, do you?

JOE. Well, no. As a matter of fact, Dr. Denby...

(Telephone rings.)

DENBY. Excuse me. *(Into phone.)* Mr. Tubb? Chairman of what committee? *(Bored.)* Yes, I know. It's the worst slum in the city. Quite right, Mr. Tubb! A cesspool – a disease hatchery. I agree... No, I will not go to the mayor... No, Mr. Tubb, our policy at the hospital is to keep out of politics. *(Suddenly infuriated.)* And I say to you...

(His face is horrified.)

What? You...you... What?!

(He bangs down the receiver and paces the room angrily.)

Do you know what that man called me? "An old vitamin pot"!

(CHARLIE enters.)

This *fellow*! Do you know what else he called me? A...

CHARLIE. A mechanical bottom jabber!

(DENBY turns on CHARLIE.)

DENBY. Was that you on the phone just now?

CHARLIE. Just my little joke for the day, Uncle.

(He starts to pour a glass of brandy.)

DENBY. Joke! Is that all you have to do? Because if it is, we can get along without you. We want doctors here, not jokers. Put that brandy down at once!

CHARLIE. Down at once – yes, Uncle!

(He puts it down his throat.)

LANSDALE. *(Offstage.)* I'll go right in.

(LANSDALE enters and DENBY practically clicks his heels at attention.)

DENBY. Why, Brook! This is an unexpected pleasure. We were just...

LANSDALE. *(Gruff and decisive.)* I'm catching a train. Sorry to break in on you, but this couldn't wait. It's about the trouble we've been having with the nurses.

DENBY. But I squelched that, old boy! They're continuing on the old basis of twelve-hour duty.

LANSDALE. *(Impatiently.)* I know that, but I've got the name of the agitator who started the whole thing. I've been doing a little investigating. I want to get rid of this woman.

DENBY. Well, naturally! We'll have to make an example of her.

LANSDALE. Name of the woman is Carrie Middleton.

DENBY. *(Stunned.)* Carrie!

JOE. You mean old Carrie Middleton on the fifth floor?

LANSDALE. That's the one. Been with us for thirty years and then turns traitor! Take her name off the registry. *(To* **DENBY.***)* I want her out of the hospital when I get back here. That'll be day after tomorrow. *(To others.)* Good day, gentlemen.

> *(He exits. A pause, then* **DENBY** *picks up the phone.)*

DENBY. *(Into phone.)* Miss West, will you come in here a moment?

CHARLIE. *(Looking hard at his uncle.)* I seem to remember an old photograph at home. You and Carrie at the Chicago World's Fair when she was a student nurse. *(To* **JOE.***)* Carrie had a big sailor straw hat, and her waist was pulled in like this.

> *(He looks back quickly at* **DENBY.***)*

EMILY. *(Entering.)* You wanted me, Dr. Denby?

DENBY. Call up the Nurses' Registry and have them strike off the name of Carrie Middleton.

> *(He starts off grimly.)*

EMILY. But, doctor! Carrie's never worked anywhere else.

JOE. Don't you think this is pretty hard on her? A lot of people favor the eight-hour shift. It isn't any crime to...

DENBY. Ah, my boy, but there's such a thing as a discipline – loyalty! We must do many things we don't want to do. Duty – we must be good soldiers!

> *(He exits.)*

CHARLIE. *(Uneasy under the gaze of* JOE *and* EMILY.*)* He's
    only my uncle by marriage.

JOE. I wonder if Carrie would go down and help my father
    out. He's up to his neck in a flu epidemic.

CHARLIE. Good idea! But don't tell Lansdale. Mustn't be
    friendly with anybody he doesn't like. My uncle *never*
    is. That's why he's Physician-in-Chief at the hospital.

JOE. Well, to hell with Lansdale!

CHARLIE. *(Imitating his uncle's voice and manner.)* Tut,
    tut, my boy! There are many things that one would like
    to do that one does not. Duty!

EMILY. You must be good soldiers!

CHARLIE. This is a big-time medical practice, Joe.

JOE. *(Bitterly.)* Sure! Through the portals of this office
    pass the biggest screwballs in town.

CHARLIE. *And* the most repulsive.

[MUSIC NO. 40 "ALLEGRO"]

OUR WORLD IS FOR THE FORCEFUL
AND NOT FOR SENTIMENTAL FOLK,
BUT BRILLIANT AND RESOURCEFUL
AND PARANOIAC GENTLE FOLK!

JOE & EMILY.
NOT SOFT AND SENTIMENTAL FOLK!

CHARLIE.
"ALLEGRO," A MUSICIAN
WOULD SO DESCRIBE THE SPEED OF IT,
THE CLASH AND COMPETITION OF COUNTERPOINT.

EMILY.
THE NEED OF IT?

CHARLIE.
WE CANNOT PROVE THE NEED OF IT.

WE KNOW NO OTHER WAY
OF LIVING OUT A DAY.
OUR MUSIC MUST BE GALLOPING AND GAY!

JOE.

WE MUFFLE ALL THE UNDERTONES,
THE MINOR BLOOD-AND-THUNDER TONES –
THE OVERTONES ARE ALL WE CARE TO PLAY.

ALL THREE.

HYSTERICALLY FRANTIC,
WE ARE STUBBORNLY ROMANTIC
AND DOGGEDLY DETERMINED TO BE GAY!

EMILY.

BRISK, LIVELY, MERRY AND BRIGHT!
ALLEGRO!
SAME TEMPO MORNING AND NIGHT!
ALLEGRO!
DON'T STOP WHATEVER YOU DO!
DO SOMETHING DIZZY AND NEW,
KEEP UP THE HULLABALOO!
ALLEGRO!

ENSEMBLE. *(Offstage.)*

ALLEGRO!

EMILY.

ALLEGRO!

ENSEMBLE. *(Offstage.)*

ALLEGRO!

EMILY.

ALLEGRO!

EMILY & ENSEMBLE.

ALLEGRO!

> *(Now the singing* **ENSEMBLE** *is faintly seen
> through a gauze curtain.* **DANCERS** *are also
> seen spinning across the stage.)*

JOE.

> WE SPIN AND WE SPIN AND WE
> SPIN AND WE SPIN
> PLAYING A GAME
> NO ONE CAN WIN,
> THE MEN WHO CORNER WHEAT,
> THE MEN WHO CORNER GIN,
>
> THE MEN WHO RULE THE AIR WAVES,
> THE DENIZENS OF DIN –

JOE & ENSEMBLE.

> THEY SPIN AND THEY SPIN,
> THEY SPIN AND THEY SPIN.

CHARLIE.

> THE GIRLS WHO DIG FOR GOLD,
> AND WON'T GIVE IN FOR TIN,
> THE LILIES OF THE FIELD,
> SO FEMININELY THIN,
> THEY TOIL NOT, THEY TOIL NOT,
> BUT OH, HOW THEY SPIN!

ENSEMBLE.

> OH, HOW THEY SPIN!

WOMEN.

> OH, HOW THEY SPIN!

JOE.

> MAY'S IN LOVE WITH KAY'S HUSBAND,
> HE'S IN LOVE WITH SUE!
> SUE'S IN LOVE WITH MAY'S HUSBAND,

JOE & MEN.

> WHAT ARE THEY TO DO?

JOE.

> TOM'S IN LOVE WITH TIM'S WIFE,
> SHE'S IN LOVE WITH SAM!
> SAM'S IN LOVE WITH TOM'S WIFE,
> SO THEY'RE IN A JAM!

CHARLIE.

    THEY ARE SMART LITTLE SHEEP
    WHO HAVE LOST THEIR WAY,

CHARLIE, JOE & EMILY.

    BLAH! BLAH! BLAH!

        (The gauze curtain opens, disclosing full
        SINGING *and* **DANCING ENSEMBLES.** *Direct*
        segue into:)

[MUSIC NO. 41 "ALLEGRO BALLET"]

CHARLIE, JOE, EMILY & ENSEMBLE.

    BRISK, LIVELY, MERRY AND BRIGHT!
    ALLEGRO!
    SAME TEMPO MORNING AND NIGHT!
    ALLEGRO!
    DON'T STOP WHATEVER YOU DO!
    DO SOMETHING DIZZY AND NEW!
    KEEP UP THE HULLABALOO!

ENSEMBLE.

    ALLEGRO! ALLEGRO!

CHARLIE, JOE & EMILY.

    ALLEGRO!

ENSEMBLE.

    ALLEGRO!

ALL.

    ALLEGRO!
    ALLEGRO!

        (The stage is now left to the **DANCERS,** *who in*
        their own medium depict the confusion and
        the futility that pervade the society in which
        JOE *practices medicine. A curtain comes*
        down on this ballet while it is still going its
        frenzied way.)

Scene Eight:
Joe's Office

(JOE *is seated at his desk looking over the day's engagements.)*

EMILY. *(Entering briskly.)* Morning, doctor.

JOE. Anybody waiting?

EMILY. The zoo is packed. Mrs. Mulhouse is in the recovery room waiting for her stomach pump.

JOE. Did you give that nightclub singer her ultraviolet ray?

EMILY. I was just going to when Dr. Charlie came in. He saw her and immediately decided he would personally administer the ultraviolet ray.

(*Looking off.)*

The lady has probably been ultraviolated by now.

(*He doesn't smile at her sally.)*

You seem kind of low today, boss.

JOE. I am. I just had a letter from a boy who used to be a patient of mine. He was going to study for the priesthood at one time. It was a sad, hopeless little letter.

EMILY. The T.B. case. You told me about him.

JOE. I did?

EMILY. Several times.

JOE. I guess I feel guilty about him. I can't get rid of the feeling that if I'd spent the last five years on one boy like Vincent, I'd have done the world more good than I could do in a lifetime here.

EMILY. Getting sour on rich city people?

JOE. No, I'm not, Emily. There's nothing wrong with people just because they have money or live in the city – nothing wrong with being a city doctor – but this crowd that we get?

(*He shakes his head and sighs.*)

Who else is out there now?

EMILY. Harry Buckley on his way through from California. Mrs. Lansdale is there too. She came in last, but she insists on being seen first.

JOE. All right, let her in... No, wait! I'm damned if I'll let these Lansdales walk all over me. Send Buckley in first.

EMILY. You mean I can look the empress right in the puss and tell her she has to wait?

JOE. You bet you can.

MRS. LANSDALE. (*Dashing in.*) I knew you must be in by now.

(*Glaring at* **EMILY.**)

Why didn't you tell me he was here? (*To* **JOE.**) What I've got to say won't take long. The other night I nearly got to sleep.

JOE. Well, fine!

MRS. LANSDALE. I was just dozing off about two in the morning when the phone rang. It was my husband to say that he'd be home late. It then occurred to me that most nights I lie awake wondering when and if he is coming home.

JOE. He works too hard. He...

MRS. LANSDALE. So I put a detective on him!

(*Taking a typewritten report from her bag.*)

It seems my husband has got himself a girl.

(Throwing paper on **JOE***'s desk.)*

Here's a carbon copy of the report.

*(***JOE***'s eyes shift to* **EMILY***.)*

Oh, she can hear. The papers'll have it tomorrow when I fly to Nevada.

JOE. Don't you think you're jumping at this too quickly? Why not think it over? Sleep on it.

MRS. LANSDALE. Sleep? Me?

JOE. Well, is there anything you want me to do? Want anything to quiet your nerves?

MRS. LANSDALE. Hell, no! I want to enjoy this! So long!

(Indicating the report on his desk.)

Read that little blue paper when you get time. It'll give you quite a kick. Good afternoon.

(She sweeps out **JOE** *is thoughtful and silent.)*

EMILY. Shall I send Buckley in?

JOE. What's that? *(Coming out of it.)* Oh, yes...yes, send him in.

EMILY. *(Calling off as she exits.)* Mr. Buckley.

*(***JOE** *picks up* **MRS. LANSDALE***'s detective report but has time only to glance at it idly before* **BUCKLEY** *enters. He is almost too well dressed. Nervous mannerisms belie his self-assurance.)*

BUCKLEY. Hiya, doc.

JOE. *(As they shake hands.)* Good to see you, Harry.

BUCKLEY. You're busy and I've got to make a connection for New York, so I've go right to it. I've decided I've got low metabolism, and I want you to give me some thyroid pills.

JOE. Did you have your California doctor do your metabolism?

BUCKLEY. No. Haven't had a minute's extra time for anything like that.

JOE. What makes you think you have a thyroid deficiency?

BUCKLEY. Well you know how it is in southern California. I keep in shape. We've got a gymnasium right in the studio – massage too and Turkish bath. I play a lot of tennis and I get a lot of sun. I'm always in marvelous condition, and I feel lousy!

JOE. I didn't know they had gymnasiums in studios.

BUCKLEY. Just for producers.

JOE. But you went out there as a writer.

BUCKLEY. I'm a producer now.

JOE. More money?

BUCKLEY. Plenty more, and do I earn it. I live at that studio! Start at the crack of dawn and get home in the middle of the night.

JOE. How does your wife like it?

BUCKLEY. Lola? She hates it. But what are you going to do? If you're successful, you're successful.

JOE. You're successful, and you feel lousy. Do you like this better than writing?

BUCKLEY. Gosh, I've got to run!

(He rises, and so does **JOE.***)*

JOE. Why don't you get back to writing? Seems to me writers are the lucky fellows. You can work at home. You have no special hours, and you have time for your wife.

BUCKLEY. *(A cloud of worry crossing his face.)* I'm having a little trouble with Lola right now. Somebody wrote her a letter giving her information about me when I was on location with a picture. I don't know what to do.

JOE. Don't let a thing like that hang over you, Harry. Get it behind you. Make an honest confession.

BUCKLEY. Yes. But I don't know what to confess. She won't tell me what's in the letter. Good-bye.

> *(He exits. JOE paces his office angrily. He picks up the telephone and bangs it on his desk. EMILY enters.)*

JOE. Emily! Is there anybody out there with a broken arm or a gallstone? Is there anybody out there worth a doctor's time and knowledge? Can't you scare us up a ruptured appendix or a pair of infected tonsils... What the hell kind of a practice is this anyhow?

> *(He picks up the detective's report again.)*

All we seem to attract, is...

> *(His voice drops off as he becomes interested in what he's reading. EMILY looks worried.)*

EMILY. Dr. Denby wants me to remind you that you all have to leave the office in a few minutes and go over to the dedication of the new private pavilion. They're going to unveil the bronze plaque.

> *(JOE frowns at what he is reading and doesn't seem to have heard her.)*

Mr. Lansdale will come in his car and pick you up at...

JOE. Mr. Lansdale, you say? Why he's the very man I'm reading about! This paper tells all about how he meets his girl and where he takes her...

> *(Looking up.)*

And Emily, do you know who Mr. Lansdale's girl is?

(Pause. She lowers her eyes.)

EMILY. Yes. I do.

JOE. Does everybody know?

EMILY. They seem to.

JOE. Well, that's the way it is I guess...

(Rising from his desk and walking away.)

Do you know what is very sad about this? The heart-breaking part of it is that I don't give a damn! *(Thoughtfully.)* I must have stopped loving her some time ago and I didn't know it – not until this minute! Somewhere in this rat race, somewhere along the line, we lost each other. But I don't know when it happened.

*(**EMILY** sits very still and listens.)*

What became of her? The dream girl of my college days! There was a time when if she danced with another boy and he held her close, there would be murder in my heart. Now she's Lansdale's girl, and it means no more to me than just another cheap little setup, like so many that pass through this office every day...these Benzedrine romances! They have no faint resemblance to love. There's nothing real about any of it – nothing real about the whole damn place. What the hell am I doing here?

[MUSIC NO. 42 "COME HOME"]

What the hell am I doing!...

*(He sits at his desk and drops his head on his arms. The lights come up slowly behind the gauze curtain revealing **TAYLOR** surrounded by a group of his friends from home. **JOE** sees them in his mind.)*

ENSEMBLE.

WE ARE THE FRIENDS THAT YOU LEFT BEHIND.

TAYLOR.

YOU NEED US, JOE.

ENSEMBLE.

AND WE NEED YOU!

WE CAN BRING HAPPINESS AND PEACE TO YOUR MIND.

TAYLOR.

WE WANT YOU, JOE.

ENSEMBLE.

WE WANT YOU TO COME,

COME HOME.

(**MARJORIE** *enters, coming softly and quietly toward* **JOE.**)

MARJORIE.

COME HOME, COME HOME,

WHERE THE BROWN BIRDS FLY

THROUGH A PALE, BLUE SKY

TO A TALL GREEN TREE.

THERE IS NO FINER SIGHT FOR A MAN TO SEE.

COME HOME, JOE, COME HOME.

COME HOME AND LIE

BY A LAUGHING SPRING

WHERE THE BREEZES SING,

AND CARESS YOUR EAR.

THERE IS NO SWEETER SOUND FOR A MAN TO HEAR.

COME HOME, JOE, COME HOME.

YOU WILL FIND A WORLD OF HONEST FRIENDS WHO MISS
    YOU,

YOU WILL SHAKE THE HANDS OF MEN WHOSE HANDS
    ARE STRONG.

AND WHEN ALL THEIR WIVES AND KIDS RUN UP AND KISS
    YOU,

YOU WILL KNOW THAT YOU ARE BACK WHERE YOU
    BELONG.

YOU'LL KNOW YOU'RE BACK
WHERE THERE'S WORK TO DO,
WHERE THERE'S LOVE FOR YOU
FOR THE LOVE YOU GIVE.
THERE IS NO BETTER LIFE FOR A MAN TO LIVE,
COME HOME, JOE, COME HOME,
COME HOME, JOE, COME HOME.

> (**MARJORIE** *drifts off out of* **JOE***'s mind. He
> lifts his head, becomes conscious of* **EMILY***'s
> presence again, and averts his eyes.*)

EMILY. Feeling better?

JOE. Yes... I'm sorry. I went kind of haywire, I guess.

EMILY. I liked it fine.

DENBY. *(Offstage.)* Joe... Joe!

> *(He enters with* **LANSDALE.***)*

Heavens, boy, aren't you ready? Brook and I have been
waiting for you in my office.

LANSDALE. Hurry up. I've got the car downstairs.

DENBY. *(Beaming.)* Shall we tell him now, Brook?

LANSDALE. *(Grinning.)* Might as well. Give him time to
compose a speech on the way over.

JOE. Speech?

> (**CHARLIE** *enters and stands watching.*)

LANSDALE. An acceptance speech.

> *(Putting his hand on* **JOE***'s shoulder
> affectionately.)*

Joe, my boy, you're about to be made Physician-in-
Chief to the hospital – youngest man ever appointed!

(JOE looks dazed.)

You'll be the head man. We are making Bigby President of the Medical Board.

DENBY. *(The hearty, good-fellow characterization.)* I'm being kicked upstairs – ha! ha!

> *(He looks around at EMILY and she responds with a laugh of bare acknowledgment.)*

LANSDALE. What do you say?

JOE. Well, I'm knocked over. I don't know what to say!

DENBY. What do *you* say, Emily?

EMILY. *(Dryly.)* Well, gee whillikers!

LANSDALE. *(To DENBY.)* Hope he isn't so tongue-tied when he gets in front of the trustees!

> *(He puts his arm through JOE's and leads him off.)*

Come on, we're late!

DENBY. *(Following them off gaily.)* I know one little lady who'll be proud of her husband today!

> *(EMILY looks after them as they exit CHARLIE comes down, nearer to her.)*

CHARLIE. What're you thinking about, nursie?

EMILY. Just thinking how hard it is for a man to get off a merry-go-round after it gets going fast.

CHARLIE. You couldn't expect him to turn down a plum like this. Being head man at our hospital makes a fellow one of the biggest men in medicine.

EMILY. Big politician, big social lion, and banquet man – not much of a doctor. He could've been, though. When he first came here, I thought... I hoped...

(She swallows hard.)

He could've been a hell of a doctor.

CHARLIE. There's something about Joe – something so *good* about him that you want him to be even better. I can understand a girl getting stuck on a fellow like that. Wouldn't blame her.

EMILY. Thanks, pal.

(Pause.)

CHARLIE. Want to take the day off and go to a burlesque show?

EMILY. I don't know. I think the dedication ceremony will be funnier.

CHARLIE. Okay. We'll go there.

EMILY. Can we stop on the way and have a drink?

CHARLIE. A drink? We'll get cockeyed! How else can you go to such things?

(They exit.)

[MUSIC NO. 43 "CHANGE OF SCENE"]

Scene Nine:
The Lobby of the New Private Pavillion

(**LANSDALE** *stands before a bronze plaque dedicated to* **DENBY**. *He addresses a group of* **TRUSTEES** *and* **GUESTS** *on the right. Behind him, on the left, stand an* **ENSEMBLE** *of simply dressed people, representing opposing spirits,* **JOE***'s memories, the principles he has forgotten, his roots.*)

LANSDALE. *(Oratorically.)* Bigby Denby, M.D. – physician, scientist, humanitarian.

     (Applause.)

And better than all these – an *executive*!

     (Applause.)

To use a phrase of his own, he has been a "good soldier." Bigby Denby has for years...

     (His mouth continues to move but the words are drowned out by the **ENSEMBLE**.)*

[MUSIC NO. 44 "FINALE ULTIMO"]

ENSEMBLE.
    BROCCOLI, HOGWASH, BALDERDASH,
    PHONEY BALONEY, TRIPE AND TRASH,
    NO ONE KNOWS WHERE HIS YOUTH HAS GONE,
    NO ONE KNOWS WHERE HIS HEART HAS GONE.
    BUT THE TALK, TALK, TALK GOES ON AND ON
    AND ON AND ON AND ON.
    YA-TA-TA, YA-TA-TA, YA-TA-TA, YA-TA-TA...

     (They continue softly under **DENBY***'s speech.)*

DENBY. Mr. Chairman, trustees, friends – the cup of my happiness runneth over. My heart is so full, words fail me. And yet...

(He proceeds to prove that words do not fail him, but we do not hear them, being spared by the **ENSEMBLE.***)*

ENSEMBLE.
THE PRATTLE AND THE TATTLE,
THE GAB AND THE GUSH,
THE CHATTER AND THE PATTER
AND THE TWADDLE AND THE TUSH
GO ON AND ON AND ON AND ON AND ON.
YA-TA-TA, YA-TA-TA, YA-TA-TA, YA-TA-TA...

(They continue softly under **DENBY.***)*

DENBY. *(Finishing his speech, indicating* **JOE.***)* My co-worker, my young but very talented friend, Joseph Taylor, Jr. – the youngest man ever to receive this appointment.

ENSEMBLE. *(In cadence.)*
JOSEPH TAYLOR, JR.!

(Applause. **CHARLIE** *and* **EMILY** *enter and applaud and cheer too loudly. Midday martinis have done their work. As* **JOE** *rises to face his audience, the applause continues and he continues bowing. The clapping hands, however, never meet each other; they clap only in pantomime while the following conflict in* **JOE**'s *mind is audible.)*

Look out, Joe!
Once you cross this threshold
The door will close behind you.

TRUSTEES & GUESTS. *(As their hands continue to indicate applause, but noiselessly.)* Don't be a fool!
Think what other doctors would give
To be up there in your place.

ENSEMBLE. Lansdale is the real boss of the hospital. You'll be a stooge, like Bigby Denby!

TRUSTEES & GUESTS. But think what it means to be a Physician-in-Chief! You can't turn down such an honor. You'd be a sap.

(*A reporter takes a flash-bulb photo.*)

See that! The *Chicago Tribune*! Make a good speech. It will be in the papers!

JOE. Ladies and Gentlemen. This comes to me as a complete surprise. I look upon this appointment as a challenge. One must approach with deep humility the task of succeeding so illustrious a predecessor as Dr. Bigby Denby.

(*Applause.*)

He has been an ornament to medicine, an ornament to his city, an ornament...

(**JOE** *and the* **ENTIRE COMPANY** *suddenly freeze in a still picture and remain motionless during the following speech.*)

ENSEMBLE. "Ornament" –
A man's brain is sometimes cleared.
By the sudden light of one word.
In the flash of a split second
He sees a signpost, pointing down a new road,
And he may take a new turning
That will affect the rest of his life.

(*Pause. They speak in a hushed torn.*)

The split second is over.

(*The* **COMPANY** *relaxes from his frozen tableau.*)

JOE. (*A different note in his voice.*) It takes a special talent to be an ornament. I am not blessed with this talent!

(GRANDMA enters, sees JOE, then calls off to MARJORIE just as she did on the day he learned to walk.)

GRANDMA. Marjorie!

(MARJORIE rushes on, stands with GRANDMA, and listens as JOE learns to walk again.)

JOE. I must therefore respectfully...

ENSEMBLE. *(Starting quietly hut with exhortation in their voices.)*
ONE FOOT, OTHER FOOT,
ONE FOOT, OTHER FOOT...

(Continuing under JOE's speech.)

JOE. *(With a sudden burst of courage.)* I decline the appointment! As a matter of fact I have another offer, in a smaller hospital, where my father is Physician-in-Chief. I'll be his assistant. I want to practice medicine again, among people I understand... I'm going home.

ENSEMBLE.
COME HOME, COME HOME
WHERE THE BROWN BIRDS FLY,
THROUGH A PALE BLUE SKY
TO A TALL GREEN TREE,
THERE IS NO FINER SIGHT
FOR A MAN TO SEE.
COME HOME, JOE, COME HOME!

DENBY. You can't do this! What'll I tell the papers?

LANSDALE. Tell the papers he's just a small town doctor.

JOE. Okay, tell them that!

(JOE starts to go.)

ENSEMBLE. *(Triumphantly.)*
NOW YOU CAN DO WHATEVER YOU WANT,
WHATEVER YOU WANT TO DO...

EMILY. *(Shouting to* **JOE.***)* Dr. Taylor! Can you use a nurse back there?

> *(***JOE** *turns and holds out his hand to welcome her. She joins him.)*

ENSEMBLE.
HERE YOU ARE IN WONDERFUL WORLD
ESPECIALLY MADE FOR YOU...

CHARLIE. Hey! What about me?

DENBY. Charlie!

JOE. *(To* **CHARLIE.***)* Come on!

> *(***CHARLIE** *staggers forward* **EMILY** *supports him, helping him walk steadily.)*

EMILY, JOE, CHARLIE & HOMETOWN ENSEMBLE. One foot, other foot,

One foot, other foot...

> *(With increasing volume and spirit.)*

One foot, other foot,
One foot, other foot...

NOW YOU CAN DO WHATEVER YOU WANT,
WHATEVER YOU WANT TO DO.
ONE FOOT OUT AND THE OTHER FOOT OUT,
ONE FOOT OUT AND THE OTHER FOOT OUT,
ONE FOOT OUT AND THE OTHER FOOT OUT –
AND THE WORLD BELONGS TO YOU!

> *(***JOE** *walks away, out into the sunlight,* **EMILY** *and* **CHARLIE** *follow.)*

Curtain

[MUSIC NO. 45 "BOWS AND EXIT MUSIC"]